GALA WEEK
A Summer Wine Chronicle

By the same author

LAST OF THE SUMMER WINE

ROY CLARKE

GALA WEEK
A Summer Wine Chronicle

ANDRE DEUTSCH

First published in Great Britain 1986
by André Deutsch Ltd
105-106 Great Russell Street, London WC1B 3LJ

Clarke, Roy
  Gala week. — (A summer wine chronicle)
  I. Title
  823'.914 [F]   PR6053.L334

ISBN 0 233 97962 X

Printed in Great Britain by
Ebenezer Baylis & Son Ltd, Worcester

To gentle spirits and peaceful places

1

'I'll tell thee this much,' Compo said. 'Rhinestones is out. Rhinestones is definitely a non-starter.'

They were in the cafe. Clegg glanced up from his paper. Compo was slurping tea through a preoccupied expression.

'Just as well. They wouldn't suit you.' Clegg went back to his paper. Compo's eyes changed focus above the steaming tea. He frowned at Clegg. 'Not for me, you dozy buttock.'

'I'm glad about that,' Clegg said with feeling.

'I was speaking generally,' Compo explained in slightly offended tones.

'I presume tha knows what speaking generally is.'

'I know you're generally speaking when I'm trying to read me paper.'

'Excuse me for breathing.' Compo decided on a dignified silence. 'I'll shut up.'

'Promises. Promises,' Clegg said from behind his paper.

Compo folded his arms three times. He began to whistle softly between his teeth. It was no substitute for conversation. He made another decision. To hell with dignified silence. 'As an item of female jewellery, in my opinion, rhinestones are common.'

Clegg abandoned a court report of a councillor and a stripper. 'Worries you, does it? Keeps you awake nights,

1

neglecting your ferrets, fretting about the status of the rhinestone industry?'

'If tha's just going to take the wee-wee,' Compo announced sniffily, 'I shall take me problems elsewhere.'

'There's practically nobody else will speak to you,' Clegg made the point reasonably.

'That's true,' Compo admitted reasonably. 'So it looks like it's going to have to be thee. There's a pair of second-hand rhinestone earrings in Dudley's window. And they're terrible.'

'What don't you like about them?'

'The price for a start. He wants locking up does Dudley. I told him, Dudley, tha's built up this big reputation for being cheap and nasty. What's tha trying to do? Toss it all away?'

'Flatterer,' Clegg said. 'What happened?'

'He threw me out.'

'That's the first time,' Clegg reflected, 'Dudley's ever thrown anything out. You were lucky he didn't offer you in part exchange.'

Ivy came through from the kitchen. Saw their heads together. Felt a moment's dark unease. They worry you she realised. When they've got their heads together. A major part of the trouble on this poor planet has its beginnings with men getting their heads together. And most of the rest when they're hankering to get their tails next to something or other. She began to slam about her duties in a purposeful manner. Establishing a tone designed to remind them of the fragile latitude available to those who have ordered only cups of tea. They got the message.

'Well, are you going to tell me,' Clegg enquired, keeping a wary eye on Ivy, 'why you're suddenly into cheap jewellery?'

'I'm not into cheap jewellery,' Compo protested. 'One look at Dudley's prices and I'm out of cheap jewellery. But I've got to find something. It's Nora Batty's birthday this week.'

Clegg groaned.

* * *

2

They were walking their bikes towards Seymour's. The usual wind was waiting as they climbed the hill. Compo's ancient machine was squeaking pathetically, like a small animal in pain.

'Fizzin hills get steeper,' Compo gasped.

They paused at the top for a cigarette and a breather. It was difficult to keep the match alight. Compo's head was somewhere underneath his jacket. His cheerful tatty face emerged triumphant at the fifth try, the Woodbine going powerfully. He gave Clegg a light from the end which the wind was buffing to a bright scarlet. They propped the bikes against the drystone wall. Below them were cold mill chimneys and the town. It was Monday.

'I thought I'd have a little extra flutter on the gee-gees the other day,' Compo confided. 'See if I could raise a bit of extra pocket money for this week.'

'Well?' Clegg enquired.

'I think I'll have a little extra flutter on the gee-gees today,' Compo sighed. 'See if I can raise a bit of extra for the week.'

The wind absorbed the words and paraded its own ascendancy.

Clegg studied his tatty companion. 'Do you think there might be some X-factor involved in picking winners that you've been overlooking?'

'Tha could be right.'

'Do you use a system or is it just natural flair?'

'It's natural flair. Every time. I never use a system. They don't work.'

Clegg digested this piece of remorseless logic quietly. 'And have you got the wherewithal for a little extra flutter on the gee-gees today?'

'That could be a problem,' Compo admitted.

Nothing more was said as they rode to Seymour's with the wind behind them passing tourist litter in the lay-bys on high moors where the sky was enormous.

* * *

3

Seymour winced at the tortured squeak of Compo's bike approaching. He was in a deckchair. Suede shoes crossed negligently on the garden table, a cut-glass tumbler in his hand, containing a clear liquid, ice and what looked like quantities of garden produce. He turned towards them with a pained expression and then away again as they drew near.

'He's sulking,' Clegg said as they leaned their machines on Seymour's wall.

'What's he drinking?' Compo was staring, professional curiosity aroused by the concoction in Seymour's hand. 'Has he gone vegetarian?'

Seymour fixed Compo with a baleful gaze. 'Your bicyle is most unmusical. There's some oil in the shed.'

'What's that in thee glass?' Compo enquired in tones rich with invitation.

'It won't mend squeaky bicycles,' Seymour announced flatly dipping his nose among the foliage and sucking noisily through a straw.

They were walking among the hills, Seymour setting a fierce pace, thrashing the tall weeds with his cane. Compo came to a mutinous halt, pulled off his left welly and flung it at Seymour's back.

'Hey up, Wonderwoman! Slow down. Why are we doing everything at the gallop?'

'I told you he was sulking,' Clegg said, feeling grateful for the rest.

'Sulking?' Seymour took a cautious pace back from the welly lying in his path. 'I am not sulking. It's merely one of the periods of creative depression which come to all of us whose talents the world has not yet had the grace to recognise.'

'We haven't all got legs like a chuffin camel,' the irate Compo said, squatting in the roadway to pick gravel from his sock. A procedure which Seymour watched with appalled fascination.

'You have to admire,' he confided to Clegg, 'the fearless way he can handle a foot like that.'

4

'That's the thing about feet,' Clegg said. 'They often don't look much to everyone else but still you see their owner patting and stroking 'em.'

They both winced as Compo stretched comfortably in the roadway and wriggled his toes. 'Well, pass us me welly then.'

'He must be joking.' Seymour distanced himself even further from the unexploded boot. 'Obviously gone completely out of his roofrack.'

'It's only a welly,' Compo protested.

'Don't be so modest.' Seymour pointed to the hapless thing with his cane.

Compo switched tactics and tried charm. He turned his best appealing face to Clegg. 'Norm?'

Clegg shuffled guiltily. 'You really put a strain on friendship. I've already passed your welly to you once.'

'When?'

'I think it was last year.'

But Compo's attention was no longer with them. They watched him applying his ear to the ground. 'There's a gee-gee coming,' he announced. This provoked a chorus of disbelieving chuckles.

'I like it. Clegg suppressed a giggle. 'Learned it from an old Redskin, did you?'

'Probably his father,' Seymour was smirking.

'I'm telling thee,' Compo was becoming offended. 'It's still in the distance but there's a gee-gee coming.'

'It'll be that one you backed on Saturday.'

'No, no. Let's be fair,' Seymour waved his cane for order. 'It's very impressive. Primitive gift like that. I think he's earned a tribal name. Don't you?'

'How about "Sitting Britches"?' Clegg suggested. 'Even when he's standing up they look like sitting britches.'

'Bog off,' Compo said, ear back on the road.

'Little-Warrior-with-Ear-Runover,' Seymour offered. Compo lifted his head and regarded them scathingly as they fell about.

'All right, Elsie and Doris. If tha thinks I'm joking get down here and have a listen.'

They accepted the challenge without enthusiasm, Compo

5

watching them critically as they looked for clean bits of road. Odd situation for a public schoolman, Seymour was thinking, down on his ear in the road. Clegg was conscious of the ridiculousness. It's going to be a big week he was thinking as he lowered a sceptical ear to the gravel. Still only Monday morning and here I am listening to a road.

They were all there with their heads down, Yorkshire Muslims in the Pennine dust when the riderless horse came clattering briskly round the bend. Three faces looked up in alarm, saw hooves striking sparks and a quarter ton of piebald muscle hurtling towards them. With wails of distress they scattered left and right. The horse ran on for fifty yards then settled to crop the roadside grass.

'I told thee,' Compo emerged triumphantly from the hedge bottom. Seymour was disengaging himself from a bramble. From a patch of cow-parsley a shaken Clegg arose. 'Maybe next time tha'll listen,' Compo hobbled towards his welly.

'Maybe next time you could give us just a hint of its estimated time of arrival,' Seymour plucked a thorn fastidiously from the sleeve of his safari jacket and re-settled the school scarf about his throat.

'Amazing how big they look from underneath.' Clegg was staring at the now placidly grazing animal. 'Like a camouflaged lorry.'

'I know that gee-gee,' Compo pulled on his welly. 'I've seen it before.'

'Didn't stop it trying to trample you to death, did it?' Seymour retrieved his stick.

'It's Early Taters,' Compo announced.

'Don't be silly,' Clegg scoffed. 'Early Taters is a small feller in a large overcoat with a maximum of two legs.'

'It's Early Taters' horse,' Compo explained impatiently.

'Oh, his horse.' Clegg considered this proposition openmindedly. 'Yes, I can see where it could be his horse.'

They turned at the sound of boots at speed trying to cope with understeer as they took the corner. It was Early Taters moving only marginally slower than his horse. They gave him

6

a spontaneous round of applause. Seeing his horse stationary in the distance, Early Taters decided to take a pit stop. He came in to where they were standing, his heavy boots scraping with the effort of braking. They absorbed the last few knots of his impact, helped him restabilise and watched with interest as he swayed there wheezing and gasping. Wind tears on his plum-red country features. Steam escaping from his dung-coloured trilby. His old khaki overcoat fastened with fraying orange industrial string.

'Oof,' Early Taters said, and what sounded like, 'Frigshaw laggish.'

'Foreigner, is he?' Seymour frowned. 'Damn people come over here. Chasing our horses.'

'He was born and bred here,' Compo groaned at Seymour's ignorance. 'Has tha never seen him with his hoss and cart? He sells fresh veg round town.'

'Blah poof sheesh wester pundit,' Early Taters managed to gasp before returning to his primary task of finding some oxygen for his sixty-year-old lungs. That done he began to hack and cough with a virtuosity which sent them reeling back.

'What if he dies out here?' Clegg asked nervously.

'Best thing is not to touch anything,' Seymour backed a further pace with the expression of a man wholly committed to not touching anything.

'He's not going to die,' Compo's voice was full of scorn. 'He allus coughs like that.'

'If I coughed like that I'd be going to die,' Clegg insisted. He looked with alarm towards the noisy convulsions at the centre of which was Early Taters. 'Might even be glad to,' Clegg added.

'He's used to it,' Compo said.

'Not only used to it. The man's damn good at it.' Seymour winced. 'Has he ever coughed for Yorkshire?'

There were signs that Early Taters was returning among the living.

'By hell, Taters,' Compo gave the khaki shoulders an affectionate slap. A small cloud of organic fertiliser dust

7

erupted. 'Much more galloping like that and tha could easily have had to undo thee overcoat.'

'Stupid mare,' Early Taters gasped, pulling a canvas halter from a baggy pocket. 'Never normally goes like that. Got clean away from me as I was backing her into the shafts.'

They were all four now edging their way along behind the drystone wall in the general direction of the horse. Seymour made mandatory signals for a halt. 'Keep your heads down,' he ordered. 'While I check the whereabouts of the beast.' Early Taters watched Seymour waddling onward in a mallard crouch.

'How come,' he enquired in a fertile, horticultural whisper which carried far beyond its needs, 'that he's suddenly in charge?'

'Used to be a headmaster,' Clegg's answering whisper was more modest in volume as he glanced to see if Seymour's antenna had picked up the inadequately damped signal emanating from Early Taters. But all Seymour's powers seemed focused on the delicate task of raising unseen his prophet's head, its hair blowing wildly. He looks like a mad professor, Clegg thought. If he ever starts a laboratory, I'm keeping clear . . .

Seymour was now beckoning them forward imperiously.

'Headmaster was he?' Early Taters grumbled. 'And by God it shows. Who is he?'

'It's Seymour Utterthwaite,' Compo winked. 'And don't let him kid thee. He's not as used to serviettes and side plates as he'd like folk to suppose. One of the Denby Street Utterthwaites.'

'Oh that lot.' A measure of misunderstanding danced briefly across the country blankness of Early Taters' face. 'Parsnips,' he nodded. 'A terrible lot of parsnips.'

'He's brother-in-law to Wesley Pegden.' Compo completed the dynastic chain.

'Dearie me,' Early Taters said. 'I bet that's a bonus for Wesley.'

'Do be quiet,' Seymour barked. 'The animal is grazing peacefully.' He wiped a sheep-stained knee on a fold of Early

8

Taters' overcoat. 'I propose to come at it from two sides at once.'

'Hey up!' Compo assumed an expression of awe and admiration. 'Seymour's going to come at it from two sides at once. That's quite a trick, Seymour, even for thee.'

Seymour experienced a moment's sinking of the spirit as he looked at the grinning faces of his little band. Monday morning, he was thinking. There was always something bleak about a Monday morning. Chalk, sweat and cabbage odours, that quintessential ambience of the Utterthwaite Academy for the Sons of Gentlemen had seemed on Mondays particularly dispiriting. The ancient Miss Fortescue asleep at the piano. The Polish assistant almost certainly teaching largely in obscenities, though how could one tell? A large overload on sick parade. Matron hung-over and peevish. The shortfall from his academic dreams so corrosive, small wonder there were Mondays one never bothered to shave. And why not? Miss Fortescue never did.

Resummoning his clan, he organised them into two teams. The two scruffiest he paired together, ordering them to stay and await his signal. For himself he chose Clegg's cleaner if unathletic plumpness and took him off in the same, now achingly painful, mallard crouch to a point further along the drystone wall where he adjudged they would be well past the grazing horse. They sat for a moment to stretch their legs.

'When I give the signal,' Seymour explained in Clegg's ear, 'both teams will rise and climb the wall simultaneously. We shall then have the animal between us.'

'It's going to be harder than I thought.' Clegg sounded dubious.

'With the horse between us? I don't see why.'

'Not the horse,' Clegg said. 'Climbing the wall. I haven't got to worrying about the horse yet.'

Old Mother Edwards was cycling home as she did every weekday morning after cleaning the bar and toilets at the

9

Seven Shepherds Inn. While downing five Barley Wines. The saddle creaking under a surfeit of Edwards she was carrying, in addition, a combined hatrack and umbrella stand, a gift of the landlord who was teed off with the way it walked into him at nights when he switched all the lights off and staggered to bed. Ma had the top end resting on one sturdy shoulder and the foot in her front carrier. Preoccupied with toilet thoughts – muttering at the state she'd found them in – the aim of seven shepherds couldn't have been wilder – she was returning to four assorted small grandchildren and a husband she regarded as the biggest kid of all. If he's still sitting there watching the House of Lords on television he's in for a vote of no confidence she promised herself. Her vision a trifle blurred by the heady vapours of Barley Wine, she was just beginning to wonder what the grazing horse was doing out there unattended when she was leapt upon by four dirty old men. Even as she began to shriek, some instinct for accuracy prompted her to amend this first impression to two dirty old men and two probables. One thing she gave herself no arguments on – they were up to no good.

Appalled at the shrieking old woman in the throes of a terminal wheel wobble, they blanched at the glimpse of powerful thighs entangled in hatrack and bicycle, scarcely noticing the horse as it lifted its head in annoyance and cantered to quieter pastures. They stood with ice in their veins while Ma shrieked and hurriedly fortified her knickers.

'It's Old Mother Edwards,' Compo shuddered. 'Though I must say I've never seen her from this angle before.'

Ma shrieked still louder.

'Don't just stand there,' Seymour ordered standing there. 'Do something.' Clegg put his fingers in his ears. Seymour tugged Clegg's arm down impatiently. 'I was thinking of more than that.' In response to this latest challenge, Clegg stole a shy glance at Ma Edwards and raised his cap. The shrieking stopped.

The effect so surprised him, Clegg remained holding his cap a fraction from his head. The silence seemed unnatural about them. They could hear the gentle ticking of Ma's still-revolving wheel.

10

Seymour assumed command. He took a step towards the tangle of female and machinery. He was wearing his best 'have-confidence-in-your-headmaster' smile. Here it comes, Ma was thinking. First that phoney politeness with the cap and now the Head Rapist with his fancy scarf and pervert's smile. She was keeping a wary eye on Compo and Early Taters. They gave her a reassuring grin. She shuddered at the evidence of missing teeth. Not a full set between 'em. I'll be damned, she resolved, if I'll be gang-banged by a shower like these.

Seymour extended a helping hand. 'A thousand pardons, dear lady, if our appearance startled you.' He bent sharply in the middle as she stabbed him with the hatrack. The alarmed spectators watched Mother Edwards rise, flinging aside the bicycle with ease. She spat on powerful red palms and took a double-handed grip of the hatrack.

They began backing away, hauling the winded Seymour with them.

'She appears,' he snarled through teeth gritted in pain, 'to be under some misconception.'

At that moment she raised the hatrack threateningly.

'She looks like she knows exactly what she's doing to me,' Compo argued.

'We're going the wrong way,' Early Taters complained.

'This way's fine by me,' Clegg said.

'Me horse,' Early Taters whined. 'It's in the other direction.'

'Tha can go back if tha likes,' Compo increased his pace.

'He's getting a thing about that horse,' Clegg scowled at Early Taters.

They all increased their pace.

The Reverend Charles Bean-Peach M.A. thrust the kitchen door of the vicarage open noisily inducing a small internal scream in his overstressed wife as she tried to wipe up cat sick without removing more of the badly laid composition tiles from the uneven floor. Finding the kitchen apparently empty

11

was an instant irritation to the Reverend Charles Bean-Peach who liked his wife to be always where he expected her to be.

'Rosemary!' he bellowed accusingly.

'I'm here, dear.' She rose from behind the plain farmhouse table, blowing apologetically at wisps of hair, a small woman in her forties, the last tatters of prettiness still in her face.

'Why are you hiding?' Bean-Peach pounded his receding brow and groaned theatrically. 'You're not starting that again? Dammit, Rosemary. It's the gala on Saturday. There's no time for hiding.'

'I wasn't hiding, dear.' She offered in evidence her rubber gloves and the soiled cloth.

'Yes, yes, yes. You can do all that later. This week above all weeks we must pull together. Where is the driver? Have you seen the driver?'

'Driver?' She looked at him blankly. It was an expression he associated with her.

'For the chariot.' She looked blanker still and then immediately guilty as if recognising that whatever it was it was bound to be her fault.

'The Roman chariot,' he turned his back on her. A tall figure, cassock swirling. He stamped his foot. He clenched his teeth and folded his arms, giving her the rigid disapproval of his back until she came to her senses. She's slipping, he told himself. My God she's slipping. What can you do? You can't abandon her. There's this terrible Double Standard when one's a vicar.

She winced at the frigid back and essayed timidly, 'Were we expecting the driver of a Roman chariot, dear?'

Compo, Clegg, Seymour and Early Taters lay low until Old Mother Edwards puffed safely past, muttering darkly at the condition of her front wheel. Then they crept shamefacedly back to the road and went in search of the mare who was still grazing peacefully where they had left her and submitted quietly to Early Taters as he patted her neck and slipped on the halter.

'Good lass,' he told her, fondling her ear.

'Very touching,' Seymour said scathingly.

'Tha'll understand his affection for her,' Compo explained, 'once tha's seen his missis.'

'Amen to that,' Clegg agreed.

They began leading the horse back to town. Great clouds were sliding placidly over the valley. The mare was content with occasional mouthfuls of the roadside weeds. She chewed on the move, very close to Early Taters' ear.

'If they've got such a heart-warming relationship,' Seymour observed of man and mare, 'what was all that damned hurry to escape?'

'Just her bit of fun,' Early Taters explained defensively. 'High spirits, that's all. Now and again she likes a bit of excitement.' He changed hands with the halter and slipped his arm round the mare's neck. The other three exchanged glances.

'I wonder if his missis ever gets jealous?' Compo speculated.

At Early Taters' place they waited in the yard while he made the mare comfortable in the shafts. There were chickens picking in the dust. They could hear pigs in a tin-roofed shed. Bees were noisy among the flowering weeds at the buildings' margins. Clegg rescued a struggling moth from the metal horse trough. The underwater in the sunlight a mysterious furry brown. The paint on the ageing bungalow was peeling. They were being watched from a window by a fat tabby. Compo was tickling the ear of a smaller black and white cat, its tail erected ecstatically as it melted around his knee. Seymour was spreading his handkerchief on a bale of hay. He sat down, placing his suede boots carefully, and leaning forward, hands resting on his cane. Clegg transferred the saturated moth to a patch of sunlight on a stable door. The smell of horse was potent in his nostrils. He looked at the silvery wing scales on his wet finger. How ingenious yet casual God is.

'He's still sulking,' Compo grunted, straightening up from the cat. God sulking? Clegg toyed with the idea. Yes. That could explain much.

13

But Compo was indicating the seated Seymour. 'He's not happy.'

'He was only recently struck by a hat rack,' Clegg pointed out.

'It's not that. He's in a mood. Look at him. Sitting there like a big Jessie.'

'Why don't we ask him straight out what's up?' Compo suggested.

'Because you don't go prying into people's business,' Clegg explained. 'The only thing you can do is engage them in casual conversation and see if you can pick up hints and clues.'

Compo nodded as if suddenly enlightened. They strolled across the yard to Seymour. He met them with a cold, headmasterly stare.

'What the hell is tha sulking about?' Compo enquired bluntly. Clegg sighed. So much for hints and clues.

'Sulking?' Seymour rose to his six feet two. 'Chap sits reflectively on a bale of hay and, lo, there appears to him a vision, in the guise of some scruffy little herb, to accuse him of sulking.' Seymour began pacing as if in the grip of powerful emotions.

'Does tha think I've upset him?' Compo asked.

'I think it's a definite possibility,' Clegg said.

Now Seymour came straight at them waving his cane. 'Stands there in his tatty raiments. Trying to pass himself off as an authority – on sulking. "Simmonite on Sulking." Become the standard text, has it?' They kept a wary eye on the cane. 'I was not sulking. It was a mild philosophical depression at the cosmic unfairness of things.' Compo looked to Clegg for translation.

'Really Big Time sulking,' Clegg obliged.

'I'll admit,' Seymour glanced with an injured expression at Clegg, 'to a sense of professional neglect. I thought they'd call upon my expertise. For days I've been anticipating the summons. I've held myself ready.'

'For what?'

'For the gala of course. They're leaving it damned late. It's here on Saturday.'

14

'It's a big week this week,' Compo agreed. 'Not only Nora Batty's birthday but the annual gala.'

'The two events are not connected,' Seymour scowled.

'They are to me,' Compo said. 'I allus feel like the whole town is celebrating Nora's birthday. I'm not what you'd call a religious person.'

'That's true,' Seymour interrupted with feeling.

'But this week it gets me right here.' He placed grubby fingers reverently over a hole in his cardigan.

'Not only gets you there,' Clegg pointed out, 'but it's gone right through your cardigan.' He turned to Seymour. 'Why were you expecting the call, Seymour? You're not even on the Gala Committee.'

Seymour laughed scornfully. 'Have you asked yourself why I'm not on the Gala Committee?'

'Because tha's a pillock?' Compo suggested. He ducked Seymour's whistling cane.

'Have you asked yourselves why they decline to avail themselves of organisational talents like mine?' He was pacing again. Oblivious now to the risk of chicken poop aboard his suede boots. 'It's not as if they don't know I'm available. I dropped hints.'

'What kind of hints?' Clegg was interested.

'I telephoned Bean-Peach. Offered my services.'

'That's quite a hint,' Clegg chuckled.

'Nothing came of it. I could tell he had some personal resistance to the idea. And I know why. Feller's in mortal fear of my exposing his own shortcomings. The man flaps. You've seen him. Terrible panicker. No gift for handling people. They only tolerate him out of some lingering respect for his collar. Fearful snob too. He's only in there to get chummy with those people at the Hall.'

Now were getting there, Clegg realised, aware of Seymour's own frustrated social yearnings Hallwards, in whose adjoining paddock the gala had always, by custom, taken place.

* * *

15

'Watch where you're going, Rosemary,' Bean-Peach panicked. 'Do try to avoid the oncoming cars.'

'I can see them, dear,' his wife replied, clutching ever more nervously at the wheel. They were driving to collect the chariot, Bean-Peach in front nagging his wife non-stop as she threaded town traffic in the vicarage Toyota. In the back seat, taking a tighter grip at every shouted warning from the vicar, sat the soon-to-be charioteer. His name was Bledsoe. Kevin Bledsoe. A retired employee of Northern Dairies, his only qualification for the forthcoming challenge his years with a horse-drawn milk float in the springtime of his career. In vain had he pleaded with his wife – the prime mover behind his volunteering – to remember that he'd been electrified for years, but she remained stubbornly non-Catholic in rejection of the appeal. You'd do it for the Pope, she told him. You can do it for Mister Bean-Peach.

Thus now he sat tensely on the edge of his seat, a small man in a Protestant car, beyond the reach of St Christopher, reflecting sadly on the pitfalls of mixed marriages. Bean-Peach took a breather from steering his wife. He turned an instant, Anglican smile upon his back-seat passenger. A bit undersized. Still, he supposed, there must have been small Romans. This one's a Roman anyway by denomination apparently. Strange how unfecund they appear at close quarters. This one looks like a fox terrier. Like a worried fox terrier, he amended the impression. One hopes he's prepared to go a bit. 'Speed and dash, Mister Bledsoe' – might as well make the point early – 'those are the requirements.' The car swerved. He turned back to his ceaseless quest for perfection for Rosemary.

She halted for the crossing in King Street. What looked like a fourteen-year-old mother trundled her infant across in a mini-deckchair on wheels. The vicar frowned. He remembered the christening. His biblical unease with the plastic names – Wayne or Duane they insisted on calling the child. The father a thin youth scarred by unaccustomed shaving. The godfather in studded leather and boot toes so pointed that Bean-Peach, in the jostling of those unfamiliar players

16

about the font, went in mortal fear of getting his ankle stabbed. He snorted, he believed silently, a nostril full of rue at the memory. It was picked up by the ear of Rosemary, super-attuned to his signals. She glanced at him nervously and with relief saw him focused on some other target. Ageing well she conceded. Scarcely much fleshing of the ascetic features despite his fondness for the heavier puddings.

The car behind began hooting. The embarrassed Rosemary fumbled a gear. Bean-Peach was twisted in his seat, glaring past his charioteer at the impudent secular hand with the effrontery to goose audibly his ministry. It was, of course, some specimen of the lower orders in a rust bucket, its windows plastered with comic stickers. It swung past them and roared away. He caught a glimpse of hairy forearms and a belligerent face above a stencilled T-shirt.

'Hooligan!' He waved less than a blessing. The poor of the bible were always worthy. This new breed, mopping up charity as a divine right, were overdue for a major theological revision.

'Ruffian,' he roared at the departing vehicle. Rosemary fumbled another gear. 'For heaven's sake, Rosemary!' he yelled at her at only slightly reduced volume. 'You've got more chords than the organ.'

Bledsoe tried to shrink further into the upholstery. Revising rapidly his Anglican stereotypes. This one as fierce as a genuine priest.

They were passing the young mother at the chemist's window. Should have been in there sooner, Bean-Peach reflected. The child's pretty head was sagging in sleep. At least we got him, Christ and I. Did the big magic on his head. Going to need all the help he can get, the little mite. And the mother. Deprived by liberty of the liberty to be young. About par for the course these days in what passes for education. Two C.S.E.'s and a pregnancy.

The town was busy. At the Co-op Menswear old Fairburn was dressing his windows. He turned away guiltily as he saw the vicar pass. A bald man with a mouthful of pins recalling the madness of that late summer fling with Her-from-the-

17

Bacon-Counter. No need to blush every time at a clerical collar. He re-set the arm of a dummy unnecessarily forcefully. Muttering through his pins. Because God sees everything – no reason to assume it gets as far as the vicar.

In the Electricity Showrooms hardcore Northern housewives were staring unimpressed at a cookery exhibition.

The road was up outside the library.

The butcher's window was Monday morning empty.

John Hanley Newsagent was ejecting browsers from his magazines.

'Bog off to the library if you want a free read. Don't come in here loitering over me stock.' He was ridding himself of two car fanatics and a computer freak as the vicarage Toyota passed. John Hanley Newsagent returned Bean-Peach's nod with the sturdy confidence of one whose bum and tit pictures were all in the rear of the shop.

Across the road, Bickerdyke's were offering Free Carrier Bags with every grocery order over four pounds cash. (Wines and Spirits not included.) Bickerdyke himself in his khaki warehouse coat – which, it was rumoured, he wore even to bed – was in his shop doorway instructing passers-by in their duty to call in and spend.

'A certain rude vigour,' Bean-Peach admitted, 'among the indigenous shopkeeping types. Pity it doesn't extend to their role in the Christian community. Never seen such a cautious lot when it comes to volunteers. Their whole metabolism falters without the stimulus of the profit motive.'

'If you're still looking for help with the gala, dear, that nice Mister Utterthwaite left his number if you remember.'

'Are you mad, Rosemary? The man's impossible.'

'I didn't know that, dear.'

'Couldn't you see?'

As they passed the Travel Agent's, Bledsoe looked longingly at some Costa del Concrete and felt a yearning to be free.

'Do that again,' Seymour ordered.

'Do what?' Early Taters enquired with a nervous glance at

18

the tall idiot he was beginning to recognise as a source of trouble.

'Just do it,' Compo advised. 'That's what we do. Clegg and me. We find it's easier.'

'Though not necessarily wiser,' Clegg cautioned.

They were riding on Early Taters' vegetable cart. Clegg and Seymour up with the driver. Compo sprawled at leisure, enjoying the rocking motion, staring at the sky, his head on onions, feet among swedes. The mare had behaved impeccably on the trip to town and now they were entering the outskirts Early Taters had started calling his wares. The first call, as it came without warning, had taken Seymour by surprise.

'Do what again?' Early Taters repeated.

'That cry of pain,' Seymour explained. 'I've never heard anything like it. How do you do it?'

'What's he on about? What cry of pain?'

'That blood-curdling moaning wail. Not too loud. Nicely understated.' He gave Early Taters a congratulatory pat then wiped his fingers on Clegg's sleeve.

'I'm calling out me wares, that's all.'

'In Albanian?' Seymour raised a sceptical eyebrow. 'There's an innovation.'

Further shades of incomprehension darkened Early Taters' already doubt-clouded face.

'Give him a translation,' Clegg prompted.

'Tell him what it is tha's shouting,' Compo urged.

'I heard what it is he's shouting,' Seymour pecked delicately with a finger at his ear. 'He's shouting – Aw God it's dead. Loomy fence edge.'

There was a moment's silence while they digested this.

'Well why not?' Clegg shrugged. 'It's every Englishman's right to put across his message.'

'What I'm shouting,' Early Taters looked deeply offended, 'is – organic veg. Lovely fresh veg.'

'The man's diction,' Seymour frowned diagnostically, 'is pitiful.'

'I'm surprised tha can tell,' Compo said, 'while he's wearing that overcoat.'

19

* * *

As she saw the vicarage car pull up outside, Edie Pegden went instantly into Social Gear One. Whipping off her apron, three squirts with the lavender air-freshener in case of traces of the breakfast bacon, a last glance with a super-critical eye over her flawless sitting room, the launching of a sleepy cat through the back kitchen door as she called hoarsely and urgently to warn her husband working on his car.

'Wesley! It's Mister Bean-Peach.' Wesley groaned. Edie went front doorwards to greet her visitors, patting her hair, proudly down the path, hoping the street was catching an eyeful of all this, a smile as wide as her spectacles, her accent fractured into its tortured best.

'Good morning, Vicar. What a pleasant surprise.'

At Bean-Peach's request and charmed to the marrow by his hand on her elbow, she let him lead straight round the back to her husband. She was praying silently. Don't let him swear. Let there be nothing untoward on his overalls.

'Is she ready, Wesley?' Bean-Peach offered his hand and withdrew it hastily into a rather vague benediction at the sight of Wesley's own oil-smeared palm.

'Well,' Wesley sounded less than over-confident as he wiped his fingers on an oily rag. 'She's nearly ready.' He led the way to the garage. 'I keep having to break off to work on people's cars.'

'Is she up to being driven?'

'Oh aye,' Wesley tugged at the garage door. 'She's up to being driven.'

Bean-Peach slapped the increasingly unhappy Bledsoe encouragingly on the shoulder. 'Well now, Mister Bledsoe. That's good news.' Bledsoe was staring in alarm at the contraption Wesley was wheeling into the sunlight. Beyond the wildest imagination of Northern Dairies it looked dangerously flimsy.

Its quiet life as a scout-troop handcart had come abruptly to an end when Bean-Peach commandeered it for its present

20

purpose. Wesley had lowered the body of the thing until it now hung rakishly between the tall, slender-solid wheels with almost no ground clearance. He had fashioned some rough chariot-shaping for the front and sides with hardboard. The shafts were just about wide enough to admit the pony the people at the Hall had promised. The Roman chariot was ready except for painting.

Bean-Peach invited Bledsoe aboard. With Wesley holding the thing steady by the shafts the little group watched the reluctant centurion, ex-Northern Dairies, step gingerly into the racy little vehicle.

'She'll go,' said Wesley with converter's pride. 'With two great wheels that size and bog all weight.' He drew a lethal glance from Edie for his vulgarism. 'She's bound to go.'

'You hear that, Mister Bledsoe?' Bean-Peach approved. Bledsoe heard it all right. There's damn all to hang on to, he realised. The top of the wheels were level with crucial parts of his anatomy.

'It's going to be a nightmare keeping your balance.'

If I didn't know he'd volunteered, Bean-Peach studied the pale sad Roman features, I'd swear he sounded as if he wasn't enjoying it.

'There's a horse at the gate,' Rosemary announced.

'I hardly think that's likely, Rosemary,' Bean-Peach began and stopped when they all heard the whinny. 'Though it is of course a possibility,' he admitted in what he fancied was a generous and broad-minded admission.

'May goodness,' Edie said. 'I do wonder who that could be. We quate seldom get called on by horses.'

'Anybody home?' Seymour appeared around the house corner.

'Oh God, it's Utterthwaite,' Bean-Peach groaned.

The excitable vicar! Seymour halted in his tracks and fashioned a servile smile. Over-hasty. Bad judge of character. Mistaken impression I'm some kind of fool. Soon win him over.

'It's may brother Seymour,' Edie effected the introduction. 'The former headmaster of his own prayvate school.'

21

Whatever it is he's after, Wesley vowed silently. He's had it. I haven't time.

It was the loudhailer. Seymour's modified loudhailer. A significant increase in volume and range, he explained to the wildly uninterested vicar.

'I like to improve things.'

'Providing somebody else does the work,' Wesley muttered and got Edie's elbow in his ribs.

'In technological circles, I'm known as something of an innovator,' Seymour continued modestly. 'I can turn my hand to most things' – fixing Bean-Peach with so broad a hint in a stare – 'if ever you should need anyone.'

'I believe we're pretty well organised, thank you,' Bean-Peach smiled coldly. Seymour's own smile faded.

'What about the . . .?' Rosemary found herself being sharply interrupted.

'Why don't you wait in the car, Rosemary?'

Rosemary left obediently and met Compo, Clegg and Early Taters coming down the path.

'It's the vicaress,' Compo announced.

'Pay no attention to him,' Clegg advised, raising his cap. 'His protocol's everywhere shaky unless he sees racing colours.'

'How's she fixed for spring onions?' Early Taters enquired. They went back with her to the cart. The one with the coat seemed rough but amiable. She patted the mare and admired the produce. Was he a gypsy? she wondered. She saw the headline KIDNAPPED BY GYPSIES. Pull yourself together Rosemary she chided herself as she fingered a carrot, you can't evade your responsibilities like that.

Seymour took the chariot shafts and despatched Wesley to sift through the garage clutter for the loudhailer. The transfer upset the balance of the already shaky Bledsoe and it did nothing for his confidence when Seymour, in the course of issuing a stream of orders and advice (designed primarily to impress Bean-Peach), began to jerk the shafts about as if he was waving his cane.

Former headmaster? Bledsoe was thinking as he fought for

22

a grip on the smooth hardboard. Not only a maniac but a qualified maniac.

'We'll have to move some of this stuff,' Wesley announced from the darkest regions of the garage.

'Have we time?' Bean-Peach looked at his watch.

'Won't take a minute,' Seymour smiled reassuringly. 'I'll see to it personally.' He dropped the shafts, impervious to the shriek from Bledsoe, and strode garagewards to Wesley's aid.

'This stuff.' Wesley pointed. Seymour frowned. Not only heavy but thick with a treacly grime.

'You take that end,' he ordered Wesley. 'I'll . . .' he began, backing away, 'find you someone with the right manual background.'

He found Bledsoe upended between the shafts being helped to his feet by the vicar and Edith. 'Can you bring him in here? I've got a little job for him.'

Bledsoe went willingly. Grateful for anything which put some distance between him and the chariot. Manfully he took hold of his end of the heavy engine block. 'Are you ready?' Wesley asked.

'Ready,' Bledsoe confirmed. They lifted. Bledsoe screamed.

They carried him gently into the house. Thank God, Edie was thinking, I really bottomed this kitchen. Bledsoe was smiling through his pain. Counting his blessings. Aware that a few squashed toes had just got him invalided out from Roman charioteering.

He went happily into the ambulance, the whole street watching his departure. Edie's pride would have been complete were it not for the presence of assorted ragamuffins with their damned horse and vegetable cart. I can't think what Our Seymour's doing. Where is Our Seymour?'

He was coming triumphantly up the path, waving something. 'It's all right,' he announced. 'I've found the loudhailer.' He put the thing to his lips and aimed at the departing ambulance. There came a mind-destroying howl from its metal larynx. Two dozen pairs of hands in the street shot hastily to cover four dozen ears. Early Taters clung desperately to his startled mare. Birds exploded from perches. The

23

teeth of innocents in adjoining streets were set on edge and the tinnily amplified tones of Seymour pierced the town clamour with his goodwill message:

'GET WELL SOON, MISTER BLEDSOE.'

In the stunned silence which followed, Seymour gazed with honest pride on the remarkable instrument then passed it to Early Taters with advice to keep the volume down. Early Taters handled the thing as if fearful for his life and hid it quickly among his cabbages.

'That'll bring 'em out to see what you're selling,' Seymour prophesied.

'Tha wants locking up,' Compo complained, feeling for an eardrum with a horny finger.

'Are you planning on doing that very often?' Clegg asked. 'I think there's every possibility I've just been sterilised.'

Rosemary was trying to soothe her vicar, desolate at the loss of his charioteer.

'Charioteer?' Seymour smiled, seeing a way opening before him at last. 'No problem.' He began hauling the uncomprehending Compo into view.

'What's he doing now?' His head still ringing, Compo continued poking his ear.

'Stay deaf,' Clegg advised. 'I don't think it's something you'll want to hear.'

'Can he drive a pony?' Bean-Peach was regarding this Long Shot with grave reservations.

'Followed the horses all his life.' Seymour patted the confused Compo rather more diffidently than the situation required. 'I'd rate him better than Bledsoe. You can't prefer Bledsoe. The man was all over the place.'

Our Seymour does talk naice, Edie was thinking. Better than some she concluded rapidly, trying to close her ears as the now fully alerted Compo expressed his disapproval of the burgeoning scheme.

* * *

24

The first thing was to get the chariot to the Hall. Seymour overrode all protests and had it towed by the cart.

'I've got me round to do,' Early Taters whined.

Seymour assumed an expression of hurt. 'Does it mean nothing to you that I went to all that trouble over the loudhailer?'

'Nothing,' Early Taters agreed but with the resigned air of one who realised his life was his own no longer.

Compo's mutiny was firmer. He sat down resolutely on the pavement outside Edie's and folded his arms. 'I'm not travelling in that fizzin' thing.'

'It's perfectly safe. We'll be towing you at walking pace.'

'I saw what it did to Kevin Bledsoe. It threw him out when it was standing still.'

'The man had no sense of balance.'

'He's got six kids,' Compo argued. 'He can't wobble all the time.'

They picked him up and lowered him still in a seated position into the chariot. 'Why are you doing this to me, Norm?' Compo asked with more curiosity than sadness.

'Because I can't bear the thought of you sitting on that cold pavement with holes in your trousers.'

'I think that's thoughtful,' Compo nodded, entirely satisfied. 'I think that's genuinely thoughtful.'

Early Taters clicked his tongue and started the mare. Being secured by the shafts to the rear of the cart the chariot remained fairly stable. Compo felt his confidence growing. He chuckled across the cart at the seated backs of Seymour, Clegg and Early Taters.

'Nothing to it.'

'Good man,' Seymour approved. 'That's the spirit.'

They were plodding up Hewitt Street, arousing a certain interest in pedestrians and passing motorists alike.

'Charioteering?' Compo leered complacently at a pair of housewives on the pavement. 'I've had worse rides on buses.'

Despite everything – Clegg was thinking – what a vein of optimism there is in the species. 'You do know, don't you,' he

25

told Compo, 'you're supposed to be doing it standing up?'

'Standing up?' There came a swift change in Compo's mood. He considered the flimsy structure about him in this new and disturbing light.

'What did you tell him that for?' Seymour complained.

'I didn't realise you were keeping it for a surprise.'

'I find you can overbrief people,' Seymour explained. 'Particularly in the opening stages.'

'No beggar,' a much less macho pupil charioteer pointed out, 'said a blind word about doing it standing up.'

'Do you imagine for one minute,' Seymour looked offended, 'that I would allow you to assume the risk if I didn't believe you were capable?'

'Risk?'

'Let me re-phrase that,' Seymour began.

They were treated to the sight of their charioteer abandoning his vehicle in a manner surprisingly nimble for his age. As Compo landed on the pavement, a pedestrian touched his arm. 'Has he got any fresh nuts?' the man enquired, pointing to the cart.

'Fresh?' Compo bridled. 'They're downright flamin' cheeky.'

Bean-Peach was waiting when they turned into the driveway of the Hall. 'No, no no,' he waved them down vigorously. 'You can't bring that thing in here. Take it back on the road and use the paddock gate. You'll find my wife there with the pony. Where have you been?' He glared at Seymour.

'We had a little trouble,' Seymour admitted through gritted teeth as he glared at an unrepentant Compo who was still refusing to re-enter the little vehicle.

'We've got a bit more,' Early Taters announced. 'There's no way I can turn the mare round here.'

'Can't you reverse her?'

'Not wi' that big pram tied on the back. Why don't I just go round the drive and out the other entrance?'

26

'But suppose they see you from the Hall,' Bean-Peach protested reasonably.

'I'll walk ahead of him,' Seymour volunteered, eager to be seen by the Hall. 'That way they'll understand everything's under the proper control of one of their own.'

Compo and Clegg exchanged a smile. Bean-Peach glared frostily.

'One of their own?'

'It's true I'm a stranger to them as yet. But when you're one of our sort – there are little signs.' He set off up the drive beckoning Early Taters to follow.

'I think the best reassurances would be to see me in charge.' Bean-Peach hurried to catch up with Seymour who plainly regarded his prestigious, social role as suddenly overcrowded. They crunched antipathetically together up the gravel of the drive, jockeying for position. Compo and Clegg shared a giggle and climbed up with Early Taters. He clicked the mare into motion. The vicar shuddered as the cart wheels bit into the gravel.

They passed between laurel and holly. Under walnut and beech. There were weeds in the gravel. Windfalls uncleared among the trees. The house, if not beautiful, was pleasingly decent. The ivy which softened its black stone grown ragged about the windows. It looked across uneven peaceful lawns between vast copper beeches to a view of the distant moors.

Seymour, impressed, was nonetheless disappointed by the total absence of people from the scene. Bean-Peach, vastly relieved, made urgent signals to the scruff with the reins to get his unsightly equipage past the house and out of sight again among the trees. He winced at the racket the cart wheels were making on the stone chips. He glanced nervously at the house windows which remained fortunately free of spectators.

Seymour too was inspecting the windows though with different aspirations. This dearth of all human activity ran counter to his secret social expectations. On the walk up the drive, neck and neck with the pushy vicar, he had been

27

confidently toying with visions of his entry into at least one of those dazzling, bustling, glamorous activities which comprise the lives of the gentry. Perhaps a marquee on the lawn. A popping of corks. A Mayfair gypsy orchestra. A little croquet at least. He stared in chastened wonder at the lovely, empty scene. Dammit there wasn't even somebody shooting something.

Compo was gaping at a peacock strutting across the lawn. 'Typical. They even have to have bigger parrots.'

'I've got this terrible urge to keep touching a forelock,' Clegg said. 'Only I'm not sure where it is.'

'I wonder where they go for fresh vegetables?' Early Taters was eyeing the house speculatively.

A dog began barking in the house. The vicar flinched and renewed his efforts to speed the little caravanserai on its way. The dog appeared at a downstairs window. It was a liver and white springer.

'Sharp dog that,' Compo said. 'There's nobody creeping up this gravel wi' an oss and cart going to sneak past that.'

A fierce old crone in wellies and a filthy hat emerged from a potting shed to glare at them balefully.

'Hop it!' she ordered.

Seymour scowled back. It was ever the same. How to get past the uppity servants. Speaks well of the family though, to keep this one on despite her deplorable appearance.

'A thousand apologies, Lady Georgina,' Bean-Peach was tugging at Seymour's sleeve. 'I've been trying to keep them away from the house.'

'Clear orf!' Lady Georgina pointed the way regally with a finger stiff with disdain and John Innes Potting Compost.

You can always tell, Seymour concluded admiringly. Breeding shows.

They cleared orf. At an upstairs window, still in his dressing gown, Henry Marcus Tyrell Cosgrave sipped his whisky and watched his mother routing the proletariat. It was something she did well. She caught sight of him at the window. He opened it politely.

'That is not suitable attire, Henry, for this hour of the day.'

28

A bit ripe that, he thought, dressed like that and giving me the elbow sartorially. 'And do come down, Henry, I require to speak to you.'

He was fully dressed beneath the robe. He slipped on an old tweed jacket and went down. She came slouching across the threadbare carpet of the hall in her gum boots. They poured themselves drinks in the General's study. His desk was kept polished. His cap, cane and gloves on its gleaming surface. The French doors were open to the garden. The only thing French, Henry smiled, his father had never abused in his hearing. A thrush was singing in the garden. There was a smell of earth and vegetable matter. It came from his mother.

'And what have you accomplished thus far today, Henry?'

Dear old mater. Always a flair for the tricky question.

'Rattled orf the odd sonnet, have you?' She pressed the attack.

'One hangs about a bit, waiting for inspiration,' he confessed. 'Flighty mistress inspiration.'

She regarded him from weathered, leathery features beneath the General's battered trilby, silvery hair spilling about the nut-brown face, blue eyes amazingly keen. Like a proud old Indian he was thinking. 'Are you absolutely sure, Henry, I mean absolutely certain that all this poetic horse manure is for you? Your father regarded it as such a nancy occupation. Is it?'

'Only, it seems, if you're very good.'

'Which you are not?'

'I shouldn't think so.'

She nodded approvingly. 'That's probably very wise.' His father scowled martially from the wall. 'You didn't like the Army? I found that surprising. Your father assured me you would. He seemed delighted with it personally.'

'I quite enjoyed it, Mother. They were extremely kind. But there was no war if you remember. I don't think I saw it at its best.'

She nodded. 'Your father had two wars. Things are seldom entirely fair.'

29

He was sniffing the air. 'I think you may have dung on your boots.'

'Oh, that old stuff.' She dismissed it from mind. 'Henry. Do you think perhaps it's time for you to begin thinking seriously about your future? You must be nearly forty.'

'I'm forty-eight, Mother.'

'Are you begod?' She was much surprised. 'Well, there you are then. I rest my case.'

They took their drinks into the garden and sat companionably on the bench which circled the rope-like muscles of the trunk of an oak tree.

'I think what would be encouraging, Henry, would be if you were to give up boffing barmaids.'

They sipped their drinks. He could hear a tractor somewhere. 'It isn't barmaids plural, Mother.'

'I have a feeling it used to be.'

'The reports you were receiving were greatly exaggerated.'

'I rather hoped it was something you'd grow tired of.'

'I'm down to one a day.'

She laughed. A brief, loud, rich and zestful cackle. From somewhere in the shrubbery the peacock squawked as if challenged. 'But look here, dammit. It's time you were marrying some suitable gel.'

He sighed. 'We've been down that road.'

She skewered him with a sceptical look. 'I'm not convinced you were really trying.'

'The options are limited, Mother. We need someone with money whose ideal man is bald, ageing, unemployed.'

'You're not bald entirely. I won't hear of it.'

'I have a fine moustache but I don't believe it counts.'

She was staring with a troubled look at the house. 'It worries me, Henry.'

He took her calloused hand, powdery where soil had dried. 'I know it does, Mother.'

* * *

30

In Cosgrave Hall paddock, in what was soon to be the gala field, Bean-Peach and Seymour were making fine adjustments to the straps of the handsome pony now fidgeting between the shafts of the chariot. Their combined efforts were largely showmanship which was clearly failing to impress Early Taters who had backed the horse in and sorted out for them the mysteries of the buckles and the straps. Now back on his cart he was grinning down on vicar and headmaster as they got in each other's way. Clegg was standing with Rosemary, enjoying the same performance. Rosemary was watching a butterfly and was content within that mild sense of well-being which came to her whenever she was not the focus of anyone's attention.

Satisfied finally that he had done everything possible to frustrate the obnoxious Utterthwaite, Bean-Peach stepped back from the pony, confident that he had stamped his authority on the scene.

Thank heavens at last, Seymour concluded, the man's got the message that his interference is childish and unnecessary. To demonstrate clearly his commander's seal of approval on the situation he gave the pony, already bothered by excessive attention, a parting slap on the flank. It shied nervously.

Bean-Peach and Seymour were suddenly as one in their haste to make space between themselves and the animal. It was a move which gave Early Taters much quiet pleasure. He watched them collide.

'Look out, can't you?' Bean-Peach snarled.

'Actually,' Seymour lied with unconvincing expressions of grave sincerity, 'what I was attempting there was to shoulder you safely out of the path of danger.'

'The only danger seems to be from you.' Bean-Peach returned to the chariot.

'You saw me,' Seymour appealed to Clegg and Rosemary. 'How neatly I was there to deflect him.' He shook his windswept head. 'There's just no pleasing some people. The man's a total hysteric,' Seymour confided to Rosemary and Clegg. 'I'll lay you odds, at school he was a bedwetter.'

'And this is Mrs Bean-Peach,' the embarrassed Clegg made

31

the introduction, glancing at Rosemary to see how she was taking this demolition job on her husband. She was tracing patterns in the grass with the toe of her sandal.

'How do you do,' said Seymour, his smile plastic and ghastly, his eyes darting at Clegg with why-didn't-you-warn-me looks. 'Yes. The old bed wetting,' he finished gamely. 'Which I always found to be a sure sign of future promise and maturity.' He smiled benignly towards the vicar.

Bean-Peach took the reins and draped them over the chariot. The pony was ready. The chariot was ready. Everything was ready. Except the charioteer. Where was he?

He was away down the field.

'Can someone tell him we're ready?' Bean-Peach looked pointedly at Seymour.

'I think he knows,' Clegg said and was drafted immediately into the little posse Seymour formed to bring back the fugitive.

'I'm not setting foot in that freaking thing. I'm not stupid,' Compo increased pace as they caught up with him. 'So bog off. Drop dead. Get stuffed. That's me finished.'

'I think we can take that as a refusal,' Clegg said.

'I think he's being over-hasty,' Seymour set off in renewed pursuit.

'That's certainly my impression,' Clegg panted after them.

'It's simply,' Seymour hooked a restrainer on the tatty fleeing jacket, 'that no one has yet explained to him the benefits.'

'Driving that crazy pushcart?' Compo snorted in disgust. 'Tha calls that a benefit?'

'Well, if he doesn't wish,' Seymour said with the air of one about to wash his hands of the entire thing, 'to impress a certain lady.'

'Nora Batty.' Compo nodded at Clegg. 'He's trying to get at me now wi' Nora Batty.'

'Whose birthday it soon is.'

'I told thee,' Compo said.

'With his starring role on Gala Day.'

'Forget it.' Compo was shaking his face. 'I've got tried and tested ways of impressing Nora Batty.'

32

'I've seen him,' Clegg confirmed. 'It's terrifying.'

'You mean to tell me you'd rather,' Seymour frowned in disbelief, 'she saw you in your normal revolting attire?'

'Revolting attire?' Compo looked to Clegg for translation.

'He thinks you look scruffy,' Clegg explained.

'Oh scruffy,' Compo nodded, curiosity satisfied.

'Instead of looking magnificent,' Seymour continued. 'In uniform.' And then he played his trump. 'A Roman officer's uniform!'

They led him back to the chariot.

He placed one welly on the tilting platform. He turned to Seymour. 'Tha's absolutely positive it's an officer's uniform?'

Seymour smiled and crossed his heart.

'Can we get on with this?' Bean-Peach looked at his watch.

First they led him slowly in a wide circle. Seymour at the pony's head, Clegg as back stump behind keeping clear of the creaking wheels. Rosemary was being talked into buying a selection of mixed veg by Early Taters whose commercial instincts were itching from under-use. But he was keeping an eye, even in mid-transaction, on progress in chariot circles.

Bean-Peach was playing ringmaster. He seemed deeply unimpressed by Compo's posture in the chariot. It was truly un-Roman. Compo was bent in a Quasimodo crouch clinging with hands, knees, elbows, everything he'd got to the flimsy headboard. The reins were hanging uselessly.

'Stand up, man!' Bean-Peach was hollering. 'Find your balance. Take the reins. Take up the slack on the reins. Stop the horse. Stop the horse.'

'How?' Compo said, clinging even harder as the chariot swayed to a halt. 'Where's the brake?'

'You just pull back on the reins,' Bean-Peach thrust them into Compo's hands. 'If you keep them tight they'll help your balance. Try it. Just lean back on them.'

'Gee-gees!' Compo snorted in disgust. 'I never have this sorta crap from ferrets.' He leaned back on the reins as recommended. There was too much slack. With a howl of

33

disbelief he went staggering backwards out of the chariot and sat down hard.

Aware of his duty in such circumstances, Clegg leapt to put a hand over Compo's mouth before his grunts of pain became a text, not even the revised version of which would be suitable for vicars. He was just in time.

'I think he's using too much rein,' Seymour advised from the pony's head.

'I think we all gathered that.' Bean-Peach gave Seymour a muttered blessing and knotted a loop in the reins.

Clegg helped Compo to his feet and stood back respectfully while he eased impacted, tatty garments from the crack of his buttocks. 'Does tha think a Roman officer's uniform,' Compo enquired through teeth clenched in pain, 'will include a jockstrap?'

'Historical necessity,' Clegg sounded encouraging. 'With all those vandals and everything.'

'You can let go the animal's head,' Bean-Peach handed the shortened reins to his charioteer. 'I suggest he goes solo this time.'

'How about that?' Clegg patted Compo sympathetically. 'Solo already.' They withdrew hurriedly, leaving Compo alone with plenty of space. They watched. Nothing was happening but they watched anyway.

'Shouldn't he have a whip?' Seymour asked.

Bean-Peach regarded Seymour frostily then turned accusingly to glare at his wife. 'Rosemary, didn't you bring a whip?'

She stood guiltily with arms full of vegetables. 'I don't think I was asked to bring a whip, dear.'

'You see,' Bean-Peach flung up his arms. 'If I don't spell out every detail. On Saturday,' he promised, 'he'll have a whip.'

'Hey up!' Compo called. 'How do you start this fizzin thing?'

'On Saturday,' Clegg called back reassuringly, 'you'll have a whip.'

Behind them, with a mischievous grin, Early Taters, as he sat on his cart, was raising the loudhailer to his lips.

34

* * *

The sheer volume of the unexpected sound stood hair on end. Pigeons scattered from the Cosgrave trees. The Cosgrave peacock hiccuped and was dumb. A passing motorist found his wheels on the grass. The pony froze with four legs rigid like a matchstick horse, while the wrinkled neck of Early Taters suffered a whiplash jerk which nearly unseated his remaining teeth as his own nag bolted. Rosemary alone was not in its path. Dispersing vegetables, clergymen, headmasters, former lino salesmen, it surged and bounced across the grass tossing Early Taters like a sock in a washing machine.

'That's it,' Bean-Peach pointed excitedly to the cart as its wheels left the ground. 'Speed and dash. That's how I want my chariot driven.'

The cart thundered past Compo. He had a glimpse of Early Taters' upended feet then the pony, infected by the mare's panic, made its own dash.

'That's it,' Bean-Peach applauded. 'Yes. Yes. He's got it. He's got it.'

I doubt if he wants to keep it, Clegg was wincing through fingers splayed across his face. He saw the chariot in a series of spectacular bounces. He saw his friend of years, it seemed in camera slow motion, achieve weightlessness and prescribe a graceless arc.

'Very ragged,' Seymour was chuckling, and visualising the judges' cards. 'For execution. Four point nine. Four point eight. Four point one.'

The film in his head speeding up now, Clegg watched vehicle and driver fall back to earth. Independently now. No longer sharing the same space. The chariot broke apart. A wheel celebrated its freedom and shot off at a tangent. The pony kept going, towing little more now than a pair of shafts and a Roman officer in mufti who had still, in his confusion, a death grip on the reins. His wellies were moving like a Kenwood mixer.

Ahead of him the mare, with Early Taters still aboard

35

though in a merely advisory capacity, had missed the gatepost by the thickness of a lettuce leaf, and reached the road. She set a course for home. They could see Early Taters' head as it jogged above the hedge. He glared at them wearily as he passed.

'If there's ever anything else,' he offered. 'Don't call me. I'll call you.'

The pony discovered the trail of vegetables in the mare's wake. Displaying better breaking than he who still followed, it stopped to nose among the carrots. Abandoning at last the now slack reins the charioteer went windmilling past, arms flailing, trying to keep his balance, and almost succeeding till he slipped on a pulp of tomatoes.

Clegg was first to reach him. Relieved as he approached to hear the local vernacular being used so inventively. A good sign. The sun came out as if on cue. A flock of lapwing settled in a neighbouring field. Like particles in suspension. It was a beautiful day. He watched Compo removing tomato.

'Just think,' he smiled. 'On Saturday you get a whip.'

2

It was the first thing he heard on waking. The steam-train noises of Nora's yard brush as she swilled and swept her flags. He searched his bedside ashtray for its best tab. He applied it cautiously to the flame of his old flint and wheel lighter.

I'll never understand how I manage that. Without frying me hooter. He put the lighter back among the bedside debris. There was only Bickerdyke's still had a few of the little rubber tits full of fuel.

He kicked free of the ex-army blanket and exposed to the morning air his smoke grey, one-piece underwear. He rubbed an ache from his knee and went to the open window.

She was moving with strokes like a piston. 'Naked,' he gasped, 'from wrist to elbow.'

Without pause in her rhythm she raked him with a spiky glance. 'Get something on, you're in no condition for mixed company.'

He grinned.

Smoking his breakfast. She flung down more water from her bucket and chased it with the brush. It's like living next door to the barmy bin. You never know what you'll see next.

He watched her planting her feet firmly in the wrinkled stockings.

37

He's looking at me legs. I can feel him looking at me legs. She turned and glared.

How does she know? He shook his head with admiration and wonder.

'Will you go and get dressed!'

He blew her a kiss. As he dressed he was thinking. What the hell can I get for her birthday?

The sky had abandoned its working clothes and was in its best blue.

Ice-cream vans went chiming early into the estates.

John Hanley Newsagent was pulling his sun-blinds down.

Young Byron Pilbeam was staining some trousers on the assumption that the Bird-in-the-Cleaner's would be wearing her see-through blouse.

The policeman whose turn it was to arrest Twintub for wife maintenance arrears was in shirtsleeves.

The Co-op were having a sale on sheepskins.

The road was up in Finkle Street.

Clegg could hear the drill as he watered his tiny garden. It was an operation which seemed to be of absorbing interest to his next-door neighbour. Howard stood there across the knee-high hedge, his moustache drooping sadly, without a jacket, his waistcoat thrown open recklessly to the summer weather.

They had been like this for several minutes without conversation. About to speak on three occasions, Howard had lapsed instead into a mournful sigh. Being thus hauled constantly to the brink of communication then denied was working on Clegg's nerves.

Howard opened his mouth to form a word.

Please Howard, Clegg was urging silently. Let's do it this time.

Howard sighed. Clegg sprinkled him frustratedly with the watering can.

38

'What was that for?'

'At last,' Clegg snarled. 'You've no idea what a pleasure it is, Howard, to hear that reedy, mournful voice.'

Howard looked a shade deeper depressed. 'Is that what you think? I've got a reedy, mournful voice?' he said sadly in a reedy, mournful voice.

'Probably only from my side,' the now guilt-ridden Clegg floundered. 'From your side I expect it sounds macho and cheerful enough.'

'It does,' Howard admitted. He glanced nervously over his shoulder for signs of his wife. 'I was hoping we could have a little talk, Cleggy.'

'It's certainly been little so far.'

Howard drew him farther from the house. 'You know I love Pearl.'

'You mean the Pearl you're married to?' Clegg enquired, embarrassed by his sudden admission into neighbourly deep waters. 'The one who nags at you all the time?'

'Of course I mean that Pearl.'

'Well I suppose you do.' Clegg found the word too opulent for an ordinary Tuesday. 'I suppose you are quite fond of her in a reticent, Yorkshire way. Otherwise she'd kill you.' Clegg was blushing. He hated being spoken to of love. 'Such things are usually left unstated,' he reminded Howard. 'Except when referring to universally acceptable objects of affection such as whippets.'

'I love Pearl,' Howard insisted.

Silly beggar, Clegg was thinking. Anxious now to get away. 'Look at the time,' he said, pointing to the church tower looming only yards from their houses. He felt his arm grabbed fiercely. It was the arm with the watering can. He submitted resignedly while the last drops of water sprinkled his boots.

'We're very close,' Howard said.

'You've got me arm,' Clegg pointed out. 'That's probably why.'

'Not us, you muffin.' Howard released his grip. 'Pearl and me. Extremely close. In fact,' he sighed, 'she never lets me out of her sight. Which as you can understand,' he took another

39

cautious peek at the house before bending towards Clegg's ear, 'makes it enormously difficult for me to keep seeing Marina.'

Clegg rubbed his ear. Not only reedy and mournful but makes you want to scratch your ear.

'I'm running out of excuses for slipping away.' Howard looked dejected. 'I was wondering if you had any ideas.'

'Not me,' Clegg said. 'I failed unfaithfulness.'

'I'm not surprised,' Howard sympathised. 'It's not easy. Perhaps you could spread the word discreetly. Among your friends. Tell 'em you know this person. A Mr X who's inviting suggestions for foolproof and preferably not too complicated ways of evading, occasionally, for innocent personal reasons, the rigorous supervision of a caring wife.'

Clegg felt his arm seized again.

'I'll pay good money,' Howard's eyes had a feverish glitter, 'for the three best entries.'

'Howard!' Her voice took all the spine from Howard's grip. 'What are you doing holding Norman Clegg?'

They parted rapidly. Pearl was standing in her doorway. The inevitable scarf worn like a turban for the religion of housekeeping.

'I wasn't actually holding him, Pearl. It was more your routine, conversational body contact.'

He's so glib the little weasel. She glared at both men – it's almost a pleasure to listen to him lie. His development otherwise remains unimpressive. Whatever possessed me to throw up all those opportunities in the wartime A.T.S. and admit him permanently to me bed? It wasn't as if he looked so terrific in uniform. I was smarter than he was, not to mention higher in rank. It's his Little-Boy-Lost look she decided. He presents this helpless face to the world. It wrings your withers he looks such a hopeless muffin. Which of course he is. If he hadn't got dim-wittedness going for him God knows where he'd be. He was doing it now. Looking pathetic, in need of aid.

'Will you get yourself in here out of the sunlight.' She stepped aside to make room in the doorway. 'You're the last one to need his brain inflamed.'

40

'Remember, Cleggy,' he pleaded ventriloquist-like – without moving his lips – as he went up the path. 'I'm getting desperate for really inventive ideas.'

Charming! Clegg was thinking as man and wife went in and closed the door. You come out to water a bit of garden and next thing you know Howard's appointed you chairman of his escape committee.

'Howard has a tendency to be a prawn,' Compo said. 'Especially when it comes to Marina.'

'You mustn't imagine I could approve,' Seymour announced in headmasterly fashion, 'of assisting a husband to deceive his wife. Except in so far as one might be intrigued by the technical problem.' He turned to Clegg. 'Did he at any point indicate how much he might be prepared to offer for the best tactical solution?'

'No he didn't,' Clegg said.

'Pity.' Seymour looked disappointed.

Compo was nudging Clegg and chuckling at Seymour's interest in the Free Howard campaign. 'Don't look now, Seymour, but thee appetite for money's showing.'

They were bouncing in the rear of Wesley's Land Rover, en route for the Cosgrave paddock, to pick up the pieces of the fractured chariot.

'And I make no apologies for it,' Seymour testified firmly. 'All my life I've had to struggle with being under-capitalised.'

'And being crackers,' Compo grinned. 'Don't forget being crackers.'

'Or I wouldn't be here now,' Seymour enunciated carefully, through gritted teeth as he frowned at Compo, 'in my brother-in-law's Land Rover, realigning my spine and being insulted by some little herbert whose grimy grey underwear is peeking coyly through the missing buttons of his shirt.'

'Dunt he speak nice,' Compo said admiringly to Clegg then turned to Seymour. 'It's too hot for fastening buttons.' Compo undid another.

Seymour swayed with the vehicle to bring himself closer to

41

Clegg. 'I want you to promise me,' he sounded solemn. Clegg inclined his ear nearer. 'That whatever happens, you will dedicate your life to preventing him undoing any more.'

They looked at Compo. He smiled innocently.

Wesley swung the Land Rover into the field. They could feel every rut through their teeth. The road to hell, Clegg decided, is paved with bad suspensions.

'That?' Wesley gaped incredulously at the remains of the chariot. 'You're expecting me to repair that?'

'Don't fuss, man,' Seymour ordered. 'You've got till Saturday.'

'And let's have it stronger this time,' Compo stuck in his penn'orth. 'Some poor twonk's got to drive it.'

'Cripes almighty!' Wesley said, poking the debris with his boot. 'I thought it was a bonfire.'

'The other wheel's over there,' Seymour pointed.

It was then they heard the voice of the peacock over the land.

They listened while the wild, raw sound was repeated from within the trees which screened the Hall from public gaze.

'I've got a double-barrelled air horn,' Wesley's voice was pitched low with respectful technical admiration, 'with boosted compression, that's not as ear-shattering as that.'

'That's it,' Compo said. Remembering his glimpse of the creature on the Cosgrave lawn. 'That's what I want.'

They looked at him for explanation.

'For Nora's birthday.'

They exchanged glances in which doubts of his judgement were plainly an issue.

'It beats flaming rhinestones.' He was becoming offended by their lack of his own enthusiasm. 'It'll have more impact than your standard dreary bunch of flowers.'

'I can see that,' Clegg agreed.

'Aren't we overlooking something?' Seymour's tone was patient and reasonable. 'If her birthday's tomorrow, where the devil are you going to get a peacock in time?'

42

'I'm going to get that beggar,' Compo pointed and set off resolutely for the trees.

They hauled him back.

'Now calm down, Little Off-White Hunter, you can't just poach a peacock.'

'They're much better casseroled,' Wesley spluttered, then cackled like a loon.

'Ignore my brother-in-law,' Seymour winced. 'It's possible too much chariot mending has affected his brain.'

Clegg was looking at Compo. 'I thought you'd retired from poaching.'

'Nobody retires from poaching, Norm. It's like there's a voice inside you saying . . .'

'We heard what it was saying,' Seymour interrupted. 'And we'll thank you not to repeat it.'

'Imagine Nora's face . . .' Compo's own was lighting up with the power of his vision. 'Tomorrow mornin'. The postwoman's been. Maybe a gas bill. Otherwise. Nothin'. They've all forgotten her birthday. Everybody's forgotten her birthday.'

'I must admit,' Clegg confessed, 'it had somehow unaccountably slipped my mind.'

'They all forgot it last year,' Compo continued.

'Aw!' Clegg said.

'So why shouldn't they forget it this? I can see her now. She'll have a face like a sour brick.'

'Excuse me,' Clegg said. 'But I was under the impression she always had a face like . . .'

'Bog off!' Compo thrust aside the interruption. 'I know just what she'll do to work off her depression. She'll go outside and sweep something. And that's when I turn up.'

'Always good for depression,' Seymour nodded.

'Wi' the peacock. Mebbe tied with a fancy ribbon. And out it spreads that gorgeous tail.'

'And just how do you arrange that?' Seymour enquired.

'You poke it up its jacksie wi' a stick.'

'Poetry,' Seymour said. 'Pure poetry.'

' "It's for thee, Nora," I shall tell her. "Come all the way from paradise just to wish thee Happy Birthday." '

43

They observed a moment's respectful silence.

'Creeper!' Clegg said.

Compo started once more for the trees.

'Hold it! Hold it,' Seymour commanded.

'I'm only going to borrow it,' Compo explained. 'She'll not want to keep it. It's like a singing telegram. You do it and it's over. You've made your point. Everybody's happy. Then I'll bring it back again.'

'Now just let's have a little proper planning here. Utterthwaite Planning,' Seymour announced modestly. 'Than which there is no finer. We were short of many things at the Utterthwaite Academy for the Sons of Gentlemen. But by God we had planning.'

'You're not going to encourage him,' Clegg sounded incredulous.

'The truth is,' Seymour explained, 'I can never resist a technical problem.'

'Nobody asked thee,' Compo said. 'I'll do it meself.'

'Has it never occurred to you, Little Scruffy Person, that you might be a shade conspicuous, trying to sneak through town in broad daylight wearing a borrowed peacock?'

Compo gave it some thought. He nodded. 'That's the trouble when Nora's involved. I lose all sense of self-preservation.'

'What does he see in her?' Wesley asked.

'She's a challenge,' Compo sighed.

'Not only that,' Wesley persisted. 'She's bad tempered, ugly and dangerous.'

'Nobody's perfect,' Compo said.

'Harold Gledhill swears it was her that bit his Dobermann.'

'Did it go septic?' Clegg enquired.

'When tha's all finished taking the wee-wee,' Compo said sniffily, 'perhaps we can get back to my peacock problem.'

'Keeping it quiet,' Seymour was calculating as he paced, 'is going to be the major difficulty. We shall need a silencer.'

'A Peacock Silencer?' Clegg was intrigued. 'I bet even Bickerdyke's are out of them.'

'We shall have to make one.'

44

'Don't look at me,' Wesley backed away. 'I've got to mend this chariot.'

'And we shall need a closed vehicle for transporting the bird.' A glimmer of elegant solutions began to shine in Seymour's eye. 'With a driver,' he slapped his thigh. 'On whose discretion we can absolutely rely.'

They found Howard on his way to the Chinese Take-Away. 'Can we walk as we talk?' he suggested. 'She times me. There'll be hell on if I'm overdue. She has me programmed to the last bamboo shoot.'

They walked. Seymour assumed command.

'I believe I may have found your solution, Howard. You were wise to submit your problem to an analytical mind. Are you ready for this, Howard?' Seymour's smile was fulsome with self-satisfaction.

'I'm waiting. I'm waiting.'

'Then how would you like – not only unsupervised freedom of movement – but also the chance to supplement your pension on the side?' Seymour discovered his lapels suddenly clutched by the eager Howard in a death grip.

'Tell me.'

'Howard.' Seymour tried ineffectively to retrieve his lapels. 'You're choking me, Howard.'

'Tell me. Tell me.'

With the aid of Compo and Clegg it proved possible finally to remove the Howard from Seymour's lapels. Seymour straightened his Utterthwaite tie and made signals for Howard to be restrained at a safe distance.

'Make him tell me,' Howard was pleading. 'It's cruel and unnatural not to tell me.'

'You should hire or purchase,' Seymour said, 'the mobile fish and chip van which is lying unused at the rear of Ivy's cafe.'

They had reached the Blue Lotus Take Away. The solitary bench was filled with clients waiting for their orders. By the

45

look of them, Clegg decided, they'd be happier at the dentist's. The only smile in the place came with the ancient proprietor to the counter.

'O.K.?' he said.

'I'll have an eight, ten, fourteen and twenty-two,' Howard parroted from memory.

'O.K.,' The proprietor said and went back to the engine room.

The walls were bare save for a Chinese calendar. Clegg studied the exotic, graceful characters. Hell of a lot of ways of saying O.K.

'Start your own business, Howard,' Seymour's voice boomed. 'Get thee out among the natives – dispensing cod and haddock.' Seymour nudged the uneasy Howard.

'Not so loud,' Howard whispered with a nod towards all the potential witnesses on the bench.

Seymour tapped a finger to his lips and smiled conspiratorially to show he understood. He followed it with the daddy of all suggestive winks. 'They tell me,' he said in what he confidently believed were lowered tones, 'that Marina likes her fish and chips.'

Every eye on the bench swivelled towards the blushing Howard. 'Why don't we talk about it outside?' he pleaded.

They escorted Howard homewards.

'They don't smell bad,' Compo approved. 'Eight, ten, fourteen and twenty-two,' he added in explanation.

The town was quiet under the lunchtime sun. Some of the shops were closed. Not Bickerdyke's. As they passed they could hear him nagging his wife. Makes you believe in fate, Clegg mused. Otherwise who's going to spend a life employed by Bickerdyke? Especially as his wife.

'It seems a big move,' Howard moaned reedily.

'Think big, Howard,' Seymour advised.

'He does,' Compo said. 'Marina's a foot taller than he is.'

'Four and a half inches,' Howard protested in the interest of accuracey. 'And that's to the very tip of her . . .'

'No details, please,' Clegg interrupted.

'Anyway, what's so big? You're not taking over British Leyland.' Seymour ticked off the advantages on his fingers.

46

'The van's going for a song. I can get you a good rate, wholesale, on potatoes.'

'Where from?' Compo was intrigued by this new addition to Seymour's range of expertise.

'From Early Taters,' Seymour frowned at the interruption. 'The man owes me a favour.'

'Since when?' Compo persisted.

'Loaned him my loudhailer, didn't I?'

Compo turned a warning glance on Howard. 'Tha'll do better buying frozen chips from somewhere.'

'Anywhere,' Clegg confirmed.

'It's just that I'd never contemplated starting my own business.'

'Thing to do is make your mind up, then act fast,' Seymour advised.

'How fast?' enquired the worried Howard unaccustomed to himself in the role of entrepreneur.

'This afternoon,' Seymour said. 'Incidentally, could we borrow your van for an hour tonight?'

They were having a sandwich in the pub. Seymour was scribbling on the back of a beer mat.

'I don't see Howard,' Compo announced from the depths of a chip butty, 'having a career in mobile fish and chippery.'

'A chap never knows till he tries,' Seymour stepped on the incipient pessimism. 'In two years' time he could have an entire fleet.'

'I don't see him as First Lord of the Admiralty either,' Clegg said.

'A fleet of vans,' Seymour frowned. 'A household name like Colonel Sanders.'

'Or even Harpic,' Clegg suggested.

'I bet he comes unstuck at his very first hurdle,' Compo returned an escapee chip to his bread roll.

'And what might that be?'

'Pearl,' Compo said.

There was no denying the force of that. They sipped their

47

beer. Twintub came in to celebrate his release on bail. They lean forward to allow his prodigious stomach to pass.

'How's it going, Twintub?' Compo asked.

'I wish she'd find True Love and get married,' Twintub sighed and followed his belly to the bar.

'What's tha doodling on that beer mat, Seymour?' Compo reached for it.

Seymour slapped Compo's hand away. 'Preliminary sketches. Peacock silencer. Mark One Prototype.'

'How long exactly,' Pearl dipped a number fourteen sceptically into the last of her twenty-two, 'have you been nurturing this burning ambition to start your own business?'

'For years, Precious,' Howard lied. 'I've thought of practically nothing else since retirement.'

She grunted, unconvinced. She had her own opinion of what he'd been thinking of since retirement.

'A man hates to feel useless.'

'You surprise me. I always thought that was something you handled rather well.'

'You shouldn't joke, love,' Howard sighed, 'when I've chosen this moment to reveal to you the hidden undercurrents of ambition which have been tugging at me restlessly inside. I have this dream,' he went on shamelessly in his best wheedling voice, 'of surprising you with a little something from the profits of me first quarterly accounts.'

'I'm all in favour of ambition,' she said finally. 'If it's genuine.'

His face broke into sunny smiles.

'Just don't ever let me surprise you with a little something, that's all.'

She took the plates to the sink. Across his face the briefest cloud passed and was soon consumed by sunshine.

* * *

48

They found Wesley in his workshop wearing bits of chariot. Seymour handed him the sketches.

'Silencer – Peacock. Mark One.'

'I knew it,' Wesley said. 'I just knew it would find its way to me.'

'Very soon now,' Seymour offered in consolation, 'when I've hit the market really big with one of my ingenious brainchildren, you'll go about boasting – I do the routine work for Seymour Utterthwaite. People will point you out in the street. He works, they'll say, for Seymour Utterthwaite.'

'I get pointed out now.' Wesley stared unimpressed at the sketches. 'They think I'm crackers.'

'What's this for?' Compo picked up a tool.

'Put it down,' Wesley said.

'Are you interested in tools?' Clegg asked.

'No point is there,' Compo sniffed, 'if you have to keep putting them down.'

'I don't get this,' Wesley waved the beer-mat sketches. 'Looks like a length of drainpipe.'

'Funny you should say that,' Seymour smiled complacently. 'Spotted it in one. That's a good start.' He got down briskly to his orders. 'Length of light, plastic drainpipe. You line one end with foam to make quite sure there's no discomfort for the bird's head. Into the barrel of the thing you then insert a few lightweight plastic baffles. Beer mats might be just the thing.' Seymour snapped his fingers like a stage magician. 'Hey Presto! One silent peacock.' He looked round for applause.

'It'll never work,' Wesley said.

Seymour's beaming features took on a chill look. He went outside to thrash weeds with his cane. They peeped at him through cracks in the ricketty shed.

'Is he all right?' Compo asked.

'At sulking?' Clegg watched Seymour posing theatrically. Genius misunderstood. 'He's more than all right. He's damned good.'

'It's about the only thing he does entirely on his own,' Wesley added.

'Mebbe we should help him.' Compo wanted no hold-ups in the Peacock Project.

'To sulk?' Clegg frowned warningly at Compo. 'People will point you out in the street. He sulks, they'll say, for Seymour Utterthwaite.'

'Bog off!' Compo instructed. 'Least we can do is try his stupid drainpipe.'

'He's right,' Clegg agreed. 'A peacock up a drainpipe. This I've got to see.'

Wally was in his pigeon shed. He heard a knock on the flimsy door. Funny he thought. I'm waiting for me birds but they've never knocked before.

'We know tha's in there, Wally.' It was Compo. Wally unlatched the door. They came from hard afternoon sunlight into the dusky dry interior – Clegg, Compo, Seymour. The air was warm, tangible, heavy with farmyard odours. A sweetness of corn. The sour of droppings. It was suddenly crowded.

'How's it going then, Wal?' Compo opened the conversation.

'It was going nice and peaceful,' Wally sighed. 'I like to come in here and just sit. You feel closer to something.'

'And I know what it is,' Clegg frowned, trying to scrape it off his foot.

'A little problem, Wally.' Seymour's neck was bent somewhat capital punishmentwise in the angle of the roof.

'Problems I've got enough.'

'Have this one on me,' Compo said. 'This problem's mine.'

'He needs Bed and Breakfast,' Seymour explained. 'For a peacock overnight.'

'Tha's got to promise to keep thee mouth shut,' Compo warned. 'It's Top Secret.'

Wally's mouth was open as wide as his eyes.

'Just overnight. In here. Nice and snug.' Compo glanced approvingly around the shed.

50

'You understand, Wally,' Seymour said. 'He can't very well keep it at his place. It's not fit for a peacock.'

'That's true,' Compo admitted. 'If I'd had more warning I could have tidied up a bit. But then there's me ferrets. I'd hate it to get at loggerheads wi' me ferrets.'

'What about my pigeons?' Wally stammered.

'Birds of a feather,' Clegg said.

To facilitate Wally's absorption of a new idea they sneaked him under Nora's window en route to the pub.

'And don't be all day!' she called.

They were just in time for last midday orders. Clegg squeezed past Twintub to the bar while Compo and Seymour installed Wally at a quiet corner table. Compo produced his battered cigarette tin. 'Fag, Wally?'

'I'd sooner have one than a peacock,' Wally felt past tab ends to an entire Woodbine.

Nice! Compo groaned silently. A bloke has one go at your tin and gets the chuffin' jackpot. For himself he selected a prime tab. Clegg brought their pints on a tray. They drank to absent friends. Feathered.

'You'll pardon me asking,' Wally wiped froth from his lips, 'but what the flamin' hell does he want with a peacock?'

'Wally!' Compo pointed to the brewery calendar on the wall above their heads. It contained a picture of a pair of magnificent dray horses.

'I'm not stabling horses in me pigeon shed and that's final.'

'The date, Wally. Not the gee-gees. Surely tha knows what day it is tomorrow.'

A slow comprehension dawned behind Wally's features. 'Wednesday,' he said.

They tried again.

'Wally,' Seymour laid a headmasterly hand on Wally's shoulder. 'Who is it that rules your life – watches your every move – and cares for you in time of trouble?'

51

'I know the answer to that one,' Wally said confidently. 'It's either God or me missis.'

What a turn up that would be, Clegg pursued a vivid image. The power behind the universe wielding a mighty brush.

Compo was running out of never very extensive patience. 'Hey up, tha's not going to forget every year whose birthday it is tomorrow.'

Wally looked at Compo with the air of one who was catching on. 'I'm with you now,' he said.

They sighed with relief.

Wally raised his glass. 'Here's to it then. Many happy returns, Compo old lad, for tomorrow.'

'Not me, you dozy pillock. It's Nora's birthday.'

'Our Nora's?' He swayed back in his chair at the strength of the 'yes' he received in triplicate. 'I thought that was August.'

'It's not August.' Compo was chewing his cap.

'I wonder whose it is then. There's somebody in August.'

They rescued Wally from an assault with a wet cap and explained to him the peacock situation.

'Well all right,' he agreed. 'But just the one night and it's out if it starts lusting after my pigeons.'

They bought him another drink. It was after time but few prying eyes could have seen the bar was still open since it was largely hidden behind Twintub.

'You don't want to be borrowing your peacock from up at the Hall,' Wally advised through frothy lips. 'They've only got one.'

'We only want one,' Compo pointed out.

'You subtract one from one,' Wally persisted, 'and you've left a gap that's liable to be conspicuous.' He chuckled asthmatically. 'Unless one of you muffins is going to stay behind to wag his bum and squawk occasionally.'

The Peacock Snatch Squad exchanged thoughtful glances.

'You'd do better at that place Him-with-all-the-Money's had built.'

'The Armpit Millionaire?'

52

'That's the one. If it's peacocks you're after, he's got three. You know him. He's got three of everything.'

The chip van started at the third try. Howard, in the driving seat, pumped the throttle, and felt cowed by the sheer amount of vehicle around him. Ivy, in the yard, stepped aside from the clouds Howard was pumping through the exhaust. She rapped on Howard's driver's side window. She watched him trying to work out its undoing. He looked less than supremely confident. She pointed out the window release catch. He slid the window back. He smiled weakly.

'You've got four forward,' she indicated the gear lever. 'And reverse.'

That many! Howard swallowed. God help us.

'Reverse is left as far as she'll go. Then down.'

Howard nodded.

'I'll guide you out of the yard,' Ivy said and disappeared from the window.

The gear stick felt loose and floppy. Varieties of arcs and spirals a distinct possibility. Howard repeated his instructions. Left as far as she'll go. He made the movement. It went the full extent of his arm before stopping. Cripes, he groaned. I thought it was going clean out the other window.

Though it had been in the shade, it was hot in the van. Odours of antique chips were in his nostrils. He was sweating and not entirely from the heat. He could see Ivy in the door mirror. She was beckoning.

And down. He hauled back on the stick and grimaced, eyes tight shut, teeth clenched at the multiple angry noises he was provoking.

Variations on a theme for chip van and mechanical idiot, Ivy was wincing at the music as she backed him out into the street. She kept well out of his way until he was parked more or less near the kerb.

'Are you going to be all right?'

'Fine,' he lied.

53

'If I was you I'd get a cushion,' she glared down at him. 'It helps if you can see over the steering wheel.'

'Good idea,' his smile was sickly. I think she's noticed, he concluded, that I'm not tall.

'Just try it for a day. See how you go on. There's some drums of lard you can have. There's a full gas bottle.'

She saw him smoking on his way. 'Your choke,' she yelled. 'Don't forget you're on choke.'

But that small residue of his mind not fully stretched by astronaut complexities in his command module was deaf and being stimulated dizzily by endless prospects of hot suppers, in his own transport, with the fair Marina and wonder of wonders, even a cushion.

Rooks were riding a thermal above them as they peered at the Armpit Millionaire's home. A converted house and barn its pale stone flagrantly new in the woodland setting. They could see sprinklers turning on the lawns, reflecting colours in the sunlight.

Nice, Compo noted. His and Her rainbows.

The limestone drive was dazzling white. A Mercedes parked outside the triple garage had its boot open. A burly man in a T-shirt was carrying boxes into the house.

They walked past on the road. The wrought-iron gates at the end of the long drive had replica carriage lamps set in the bright, new stone. An ornate, metal name-plate identified the house as 'Harbour Lights'.

'A hundred miles from the sea,' Clegg said. 'They must be some lights.'

'He's a boating type,' Seymour explained. 'All self-made millionaires are boating types. The sea is in every rich Englishman's blood.'

'No swimming pool,' Compo sneered. 'That's very similar to my house.'

'It's probably indoors,' Seymour mopped his brow with a spotless, Edie-laundered handkerchief. 'There aren't many days as hot as this for swimming outside.'

'Indoors,' Clegg said. 'Poor devil. That must have been a

terrible decision. Having to put it where it wouldn't show.'

Something small and pedigree which belonged to the Armpit Millionaire's wife began to yap as they passed.

'Hey up,' Compo grinned. 'These premises are protected by a guard dog. I've had ferrets bigger than that.'

'It's noisy,' Clegg warned. 'There could be a commotion if it got up your trouser leg.'

Like a spring-loaded fluffy toy the game little thing was lurching forward with the force of every yap. The T-shirt man came out of the house and stared at them on the road.

'Is that him?' Compo asked.

'I expect so,' Seymour frowned. 'He looks very much, to me, like someone who's made a fortune selling cut-price deodorants to market traders.'

They passed a field where a pony was grazing and then the trees began. The narrow road became pinched even further as it crossed a little stone bridge. Beyond the bridge the road curved right and began to climb gently. Compo and Clegg carried their jackets. Seymour retained his lightweight summer linen. The road followed the curves of a little river. It pinballed cheerfully between the larger stones and marked the boundary of the property of the Armpit Millionaire. Across the river were the trees. The house was here completely concealed. Seymour stopped them with his cane and pointed. As if in a spotlight, among the darker trees a splendid peacock was scratching in a patch of sunlight. It saw them and flourished proudly. It raised its head and shrieked.

'Hey up,' Compo said admiringly. 'That's the beggar for me.'

'And this is the place,' Seymour weighed the advantages. 'Park the chip van in the lay-by here. Out with a ladder. Use it to cross the river. Off with our peacock net into the trees.'

'All in the dark?' Clegg sounded unenthusiastic.

'It's never fully dark,' Seymour said confidently. 'Not at this time of year.'

Clegg scowled at Compo. 'Why the heck can't you just buy her a birthday card?'

* * *

55

They went to the cafe for Ivy's cool, home-made lemonade and to pick up what rumours they could of Howard and the chip van. Ivy was too sharp to interrogate safely. They waited until her back was turned and they could take a crack at Crusher.

He came in through the street door like a forklift truck in a white apron. He was carrying armfuls of the heavy tinned staples of the catering trade as if they were weightless.

'How do, Crush,' Compo greeted.

Crusher's amiable face assumed its second expression as it switched from habitual mild confusion to a happy grin. 'How do,' he said and took his load into the kitchen.

'And that's the last clear answer we'll get from him,' Seymour sighed.

'He does his best,' Compo sprang to the defence. 'He's a good lad.'

'But not entirely reliable as a source of information.'

'Why are we talking in guilty whispers?' Clegg answered his own question. 'I'll tell you why we're talking in guilty whispers. Because we're feeling guilty.'

'I'm not feeling guilty,' Compo asserted.

'Well you should be,' Clegg insisted. 'There could be very severe penalties for removing a peacock without its owner's consent.'

'Keep your voice down.' Seymour looked towards the kitchen nervously.

'You see,' Clegg indicated Seymour. 'He's feeling guilty.'

'Not exactly guilty. It's more your operational caution.'

'I've never heard such a pair of old tulips in me life,' Compo snorted. 'We're not nicking it for the pot.'

'Exactly,' Seymour concurred. 'We're simply borrowing the creature. It gets a little exercise. It brings a little birthday happiness to a drab life.'

'Drab?' Compo protested. 'She lives next door to me. That's not drab. That's dicing forever on the edge of romance and excitement.'

'I stand corrected,' Seymour rolled his eyes. 'You must understand, Clegg, my own position in this affair. Would I be in it for any improper motive? No,' he said hastily to beat any frivolous replies. 'It happens to be my conviction that I may have stumbled here on to something worth pursuing. Peacocks for a lady's birthday. It could become the fashionable thing. It has a certain glamour. It could catch on. Imagine if I could corner a modest royalty on every peacock displayed on every birthday . . .' Seymour's eyes were aglitter with peacock dreams.

'Thee corner?' Compo pierced the bubble. 'Just slow down a minute, Big Alice, it were my idea.'

'Oh all right,' Seymour snarled. 'If we all could corner a modest royalty.' He reset his features into a semblance of sweet reason. 'You see, Clegg, my interest here is, very properly, to monitor the scheme for its commercial possibilities.'

'Right,' Compo agreed.

They looked at Clegg.

'I'd feel much better,' he said, 'if we just asked the bloke could we borrow his peacock.'

They sighed. Compo pushed back his chair and got to his feet. 'Tell thee what,' he settled his knitted cap to a determined angle. 'Why don't we go and ask the bloke if we can borrow his peacock?'

'I've been thinking,' Compo said as they started out for 'Harbour Lights'. 'About that uniform. That Roman officer's uniform. It better really look swank if I've got to drive that two-wheeled death trap.'

'It's not a death trap,' Seymour scoffed.

'Not for thee,' Compo pointed out. 'The only thing tha'll be driving is thee mouth as usual.'

'I promised the vicar you'd drive,' Seymour frowned. 'You can't let people down.'

'It very much depends,' Compo announced flatly, 'on that uniform. Is it going to be a Nora Batty puller or is it?'

They made a detour to the library to show him a picture.

57

'Roman officers,' Seymour flicked through the pages, 'looked magnificent.'

'Are you ready for magnificent?' Clegg queried.

'I am, Norm,' Compo said.

'There you are.' Seymour passed the page to Compo. 'Roman centurion. Magnificent.'

'Oh great,' he groaned. 'No trousers. Just this dinky little pinny.' He left in deflated mood. They scrambled in pursuit but he was immovable. If he couldn't do it in trousers he wasn't doing it.

'They didn't have trousers,' Seymour argued. 'And yet they made the world tremble.'

'They never met Nora Batty,' Compo said.

They were hot and tired as they came over the brow of the hill and saw the Armpit Millionaire's place in the distance.

'A few more times,' Seymour panted sarcastically, 'and we're going to be used to this hill.'

'I'm gagging,' Compo wheezed.

'Nobody said,' Clegg was puffing, 'doing the right thing had to be easy.' A comment which brought him several minutes of their touchy silence.

Seymour's hot and scarlet features were moving expressively through images of doubt. 'The problem is,' he broke the silence finally. 'What are we going to tell him we want the creature for?'

'Nora's birthday.' Compo saw no problem.

'I think what Compo's suggesting,' Clegg removed his cap and fanned his forehead, 'is that we start getting really sneaky and tell him the truth.'

'You fools!' Seymour's arms and cane were wagging excitedly.

They ducked and backed out of danger. The meaning was inescapable. He was semaphoring a very resolute No.

'The truth!' Seymour was truly appalled.

'Sorry,' Compo apologised.

'No harm intended,' Clegg flinched.

'So he can steal my idea?' Seymour's eyes rolled heavenwards. 'And corner for himself the Birthday Peacock Market?'

Heaven remained unruffled by the news. The sky stayed blue, serene, indifferent. 'Be fair,' Seymour challenged it. 'Who invented the silencer? What does he need with my peacocks? Let him stick to armpits.'

Old Testament prophet, Clegg was thinking. Seymour looked the part. Hair wild, eyes wilder.

'I was under the impression,' Compo sniffed haughtily, 'that Birthday Peacocks was all my idea.'

'I think,' Clegg explained, 'that quite early on in that career you became the subject of a takeover.'

'Right,' Seymour got them back on the march. 'Now we've got the frivolous objections out of the way, what are we going to tell him?'

The Mercedes was still in the drive. Its boot closed now.

'It's not as if we're lying.' Seymour stabbed Clegg for encouragement with his cane. 'A little commercial smokescreen. An inventor has to have his secrets. We all do it. The nuclear chaps. The space labs. I.C.I. Me.'

'Oh well,' Clegg said. 'If it's for national security.'

'O.K., Big Gob,' Compo passed the ball to Seymour. 'Tell us. Why would three blokes appear out the blue, desperate to borrow a peacock?'

This brought them to a halt again, now only yards from the entrance to the drive. A tractor passed towing an implement. The thin face of the youth in the cab squeezed between stereo earphones. It went over the little bridge.

'Could we tell him,' Compo suggested, 'that we have this old relative what's about to snuff it . . .'

'Old silver-haired, dying relative,' Clegg said, getting the picture. 'With work-worn hands and a spotlessly clean pinny, whose last simple wish . . .'

'Is to see a peacock,' Compo finished.

'Too morbid,' Seymour shook his head.

They thought again.

'We could be keen amateur painters,' Clegg offered. 'Come to borrow it to paint it.'

'I think it's a great colour already,' Compo cackled. They made him face the other way.

'It's all too fanciful,' Seymour took one of his famous firm grips on the situation. 'Quite unnecessary.' He smoothed back his straying hair, readjusted the hang of a now rather heat-dishevelled linen jacket and struck his Pillar of the Establishment pose. 'As principal and proprietor of the Utterthwaite Postal University I have a certain prestige.'

'No pupils,' Compo said. 'Just prestige.'

'I've explained that before,' Seymour snarled. 'The education business is seasonal. And the fact remains that it's only too reasonable,' he waved his cane airily in the direction of the house, 'that I should turn up at this chap's door requiring the loan of his peacock for teaching purposes.'

'All very well,' Compo looked pessimistic, 'but tha'll be in trouble if he says he dunt want his peacock teaching.'

'Let me do the talking,' Seymour ordered.

'No problem,' Compo said. 'It's stopping thee that's difficult.'

An eight-year-old opened the door. She was wearing make-up and eating a multi-coloured ice cream. 'I've got a pony,' she said. 'My daddy's rich.'

Her mother appeared, clucking with embarrassment. 'Angelica, I've told you never to say that.' She smiled apologetically. 'Say wealthy.' The dog in her arms was yapping a shrill staccato which effectively scrambled Seymour's opening speech.

She was young and bleached. Barefoot almost to the waist in a denim mini. She stared at Seymour uncomprehendingly. 'Hang on,' she said and disappeared into the cool interior.

There was a hi-fi throbbing. The dog still yapping. They live high on the decibels, Clegg was thinking, in the deodorant belt. They waited outside the door. Angelica returned for a moment to stare.

'Give us a lick,' Compo winked.

She turned expressionless and left.

'Have you always been good with children?' Clegg asked.

'It's just a gift,' Compo said.

The woman returned without the dog. She had three pound notes. 'Here you are,' she said. 'Don't tell my husband. And get yourselves a bed. Don't spend it on booze.' She shut the door before they could speak. They were still gaping at the notes.

'I have never,' Seymour flung his pound to the floor, 'been so insulted in all my days.'

'Oh I have,' Compo said, retrieving Seymour's pound.

'Ring the bell,' Seymour ordered Clegg. 'And give me that.' He made a grab for Compo's two pound notes.

'Finders keepers.' Compo whipped them to safety behind his back.

'Ring the bell, the money must go back.'

'Point of order,' Compo protested. 'Tha can't go throwing charity in people's faces.'

'You ring the bell,' Clegg stepped back from the doorway. 'I don't like messing with things electric.'

Seymour raked his motley crew with a disaffected eye and stepped magnificently to the bell. This time the door was opened with a vigorous heave by the Armpit Millionaire himself. He glared at Seymour's finger on the bell.

No doubt he gets everything wholesale, Clegg was thinking, but that's still a lot of muscle under that T-shirt. Seymour was reaching similar conclusions. He stepped back apace. The face was pugnacious. The hair styled and blow-waved. The Armpit Millionaire looked like a guard dog in show condition.

'I told her,' he snarled, 'you'd be back for more. But God Almighty not this quick.' He took handfuls of the first two collars he could reach. They belonged to Seymour and the startled Clegg. They found themselves being propelled down the drive by what felt like a small crane.

Compo picked up the third pound note, dropped by Clegg in his panic, whose mind — not to mention the neck of his jacket — was rising far above money matters.

Stifling his giggles, Compo rejoined them on the road, their

61

faces crimson. The Armpit Millionaire was watching from his gate.

'And what did he say then?' Compo's face was unconvincing with simulated innocence. 'When they asked him for a loan of his peacock?' He leapt nimbly from the reach of Seymour's stick.

'If ever a bloke,' Clegg was struggling to reslacken the knot of his tie, 'needed his peacock surreptitiously borrowing, it's him.'

They were tired and hungry when they got back to town. They called at Bickerdyke's for boiled ham cut from the bone. 'Nice and thick,' Clegg ordered. Bickerdyke groaned. Faddy customers. He sharpened his knife and yearned nostalgically for the great days of rationing and the war.

They went to Clegg's for tea. The chip van was parked in the street. Howard was fussing about with the burners. Pearl was staring from her front step. 'Just what we needed,' she said as they filed into Clegg's. 'An eyesore we can park outside the door.'

Howard came in halfway through tea. 'I'm just about ready,' he announced, 'for me maiden voyage.'

'If it's maidens tha's after,' Compo said with his mouth full. 'That's going to disqualify Marina.'

Howard consoled himself with a chocolate biscuit. 'She explained all that,' he pouted. 'We have no secrets. It was him she was engaged to all those years. He let her down badly.'

They were sniffing the air. It was Howard.

'Howard,' Clegg pointed out, 'you've only had it five minutes. You smell of chips already.'

'I know. That's what Pearl said. Not – let me be the first to wish you all the best with your brave new enterprise – you'll notice. Not – Oh, Howard, I think it's terrific that you're taking this commercial plunge – just – You smell of chips.' He helped himself to another biscuit.

'Have a biscuit, Howard,' Clegg said.

62

'Right,' Seymour wiped his lips with a best Clegg linen napkin. 'Down to business. And the co-ordination of our activities.' He pointed a finger at Howard. 'Where are you planning on starting your chip round?'

'I don't know,' Howard whined as he slumped sadly into a chair. 'Decisions! That's all I've done all day since starting me own business.'

'Your tea's ready!' Edie called. The hammering in the workshop continued. Switching to boost she tried again. 'Wesley, your tea's on the table.' She caught sight of Mrs Fothergill passing in the street. Patting her hair and reducing her volume to dulcet, Edie smiled a greeting. 'A nace fine day we're having, Mrs Fothergill.'

Mrs Fothergill began crossing the street to have a word. Edie went to meet her at the gate. Mrs Fothergill shrieked at being narrowly missed by an approaching chip van which seemed determined to park at her feet.

Howard smiled apologetically behind the wheel. The two women stared.

'Who ordered chips?' Edie shrugged with embarrassment at Mrs Fothergill. 'Aym sure there's no demand for mobile catering at this house.'

'Take it away,' she snarled at Howard and was alarmed to see the whole vehicle suddenly disgorging passengers one of whom was her brother Seymour.

'Good evening, Edith.' He doffed his hat to the two women.

He's got lovely manners, Our Seymour, Edie was thinking. But what is he doing emerging from such a vehicle?

Clegg touched his cap, Compo grinned and winked and they followed Seymour into Wesley's workshop.

'Wasn't that your Seymour?'

That's the trouble with Mrs Fothergill, Edie decided. Nosy old witch.

'Someone very lake,' she admitted. 'Well. Must be off.

63

Toodleoo, Mrs Fothergill.' Edie scurried back into the house to await the departure of the intruder.

'I like it,' Seymour admired the peacock silencer. He felt the foam padding. 'Yes. That should be very comfortable.'

'Head up a drainpipe,' Compo said. 'Bound to be comfortable.'

'It's the same principle,' Seymour explained, 'as placing a cover over a cage. The bird finds the darkness soothing.'

It had the shape of a golf club. The short bit was the padded end which then curved quickly to a vertical.

'It's a bit long.' Clegg was frowning. 'I was expecting something – daintier.'

Wesley was offended. 'It's for a peacock not a fizzin budgie.'

'There's a lot of sound to deaden,' Seymour lectured technically. 'One needs sufficient length of baffle chamber.'

'Once tha sticks its head in there it should baffle the beggar,' Compo agreed.

'But does it work?' Clegg was not optimistic.

They stepped outside to test it. In the house, Edie was watching behind her net curtains. What are they doing? she wondered. Why is Our Seymour putting a drainpipe to his lips? She felt a twinge of sadness for him. Will retirement suit him? Will he cope with the reduction in his social circumstances? He never used to put drainpipes to his lips.

Seymour's face was turning red. He took a deep breath and bellowed a further experimental howl into the silencer. Those about him could hear the muffled noises of Seymour up a drainpipe. Behind her window, Edie could hear no sound. Poor Seymour, she sympathised – he's invented a musical instrument – superbly simple in design – and judging by the look of it at a price well within the reach of even the shabbiest

64

musical pocket and, wouldn't you know it, he can't get the damn thing to play. Thank God Mrs Fothergill isn't here to witness his humiliation. A chip van and a failed musical drainpipe all in one day. Poor Seymour. She made a cup of tea. She heard the chip van depart. Wesley came in for his tea.

'And don't think you're sitting down in them mucky overalls.'

While he washed she was clattering about. A sure sign of indignation. In good moods she could move like a cat. 'I hate Our Seymour being reduced to riding in chip vans. It's no kind of conveyance for a sensitive soul whose fondest wish is to provide music cheaply for the masses.'

He felt for the towel. 'What the hell is she on about?' he wondered.

'You're driving like a pillock, Howard,' said the sensitive soul whose fondest wish it was to provide music cheaply for the masses. He was seated next to the perspiring driver. Clegg and Compo were having their teeth rattled in the back.

'It's all new to me,' Howard bleated. 'Mebbe I should have brought two cushions.' Yes. That's it, he decided, a delicious sliver of wickedness piercing for a second the leaden lump of anxiety in his bowels. Next time I'll bring two cushions.

Acting under Seymour's instructions Howard dropped them off at the Seven Shepherds. It was just past opening time.

'You will return for us here,' Seymour explained in head-masterly tones adapted for consumption by a six-year-old, 'as soon as it becomes decently dusk. I am leaving the silencer in your charge. Also Wesley's ladder on your roof.'

'Great,' Howard whined. 'Just what I need. More responsibility.'

'The rest of the evening is yours,' Seymour waved his cane munificently as if solely responsible for the warm mellow evening it was. 'Begin building your business. Go spread cholesterol about the villages.' He lowered his voice and stuck

65

his head inside the door. 'We shall find occasion later to discuss the terms of my commission.'

'And give our regards to Marina,' Compo cackled, nudging Clegg.

'Don't be like that,' the blushing Howard protested. 'Where's the harm in a chip van proprietor having to turn to someone for a little catering assistance?'

They watched him go on his way, nose in the air, narrowly missing a car as it turned into the pub forecourt.

'Who was that prat?' enquired the angry driver.

'Never saw him before in our lives,' Clegg shrugged. 'Just chips that pass in the night.'

The landlord looked up from his newspaper spread on the bar.

Seymour raised his cane in salute. 'Greetings, landlord!'

Oh God! The landlord sighed. The pitfalls of the pub trade. 'You!' he pointed to Compo. 'First sign of a ferret and you're barred.'

'I'm clean,' Compo grinned, showing his pocket linings.

Clean? The landlord shuddered. Not the first word that springs to mind. He pulled their pints. 'Can you hide him in a corner,' he pleaded. 'He can murder the bar-food trade.'

'Better yet,' Seymour smiled reassuringly. 'On this bonny evening we shall take our drinks outside.'

'Round the back's nice,' the landlord said quickly. 'He'll enjoy it much better than where they can see him when they turn in the car park.'

Marina's face in the mirror was frozen as if in a scream. What she was doing was attaching a false eyelash. She blinked a few times rapidly to check its alignment with the rest of her equipment. The face that stared back at her though not unattractive was past its prime. But she was a trier. This much

66

was evident in the care with which she applied too much make-up. And in the elaborate back-combing of the dyed and fussy hair. Regimented with lacquer it was like the spun-sugar the kids would be buying at Saturday's gala.

Happy at last with the mask her art had created she rose from her dressing table and pulled on a freshly laundered crisply ironed blouse. Semi-transparent. A quality for which she felt a natural affinity in any flimsy material.

'Bring a white apron,' the note had said, slipped to her at the supermarket check-out counter where she worked part time. Passed by Howard in dark glasses overacting his role of perfect stranger. Dropping his change. Departing scarlet-faced with the single item in his trolley he always purchased as a cover for these emergencies. A pack of Rhino Brand medium-fine emery paper.

'Howard,' she had asked him one night while they were holding hands timidly in the deepest shadows of the warmest wall at the rear of Ackroyd's Bakery. 'Why do you always buy a pack of Rhino Brand medium-fine emery paper?'

'It's not just a whim,' he had explained. The slight tremor in his voice their stolen moments always aroused in him. 'It's something I had to calculate carefully. It had to be something a man, alone, in a supermarket could feel comfortable with. In case I was ever observed it had to look natural. It had to be masculine. It had to be free of any' – and here he had swallowed and she had felt his grip on her fingers tighten – 'extra-marital undertones. I daren't risk after-shave or scented soap. I felt even toothpaste was border-line. You keep nipping in for excessive Colgate and somebody's going to start wondering. So it had to be something above suspicion. I know they laugh at me in the supermarket. That Howard. With his emery paper. I laugh at them laughing at me. What do I care? As long as I can keep from compromising you.'

He was so thoughtful. She had given him a squeeze. 'Oh God!' he had clutched her with surprising vigour. 'If only the world would understand a man's needs. If only we could come out in the open. I hate hiding our love behind sheets of Rhino Brand medium-fine emery paper.'

67

And he had pressed her tenderly against the bakery wall. The following morning at breakfast her sister had noticed the brick dust on the navy-blue costume.

'It's better than dandruff,' Marina had said.

And now, in her bedroom, she re-read Howard's latest communication.

Written on a piece of outer wrapping from a pack of Rhino Brand medium-fine emery paper, in the always identical childish capitals by which Howard tried to conceal his natural hand, it read:

'My love. At last we have our own transport. With ample room in the back. I am going into business. We shall have more time together. Be at the corner near Bickerdyke's at 7.45. Bring a white apron. I love you. A friend.'

What business? And why a white apron? White? The colour for maidens. Brides? Her hand, the nails the colour of burgundy, flew to a suddenly pounding heart. What was he up to with his bridal white? Despite his marital status. Was he bent on taking her into the hills in his own transport? For some pagan facsimile of wedlock?

She sat down weakly on the bed.

The car park was filling at the Seven Shepherds. They were at a table in the beer garden. The distant hills were darkening with the lowering sun. It was still warm.

Compo's head went back as he emptied his glass. 'I'll get these,' he said as he came up for air. He flashed the three pound notes.

They winced at the memory.

'Money's money,' Compo grinned.

'We shall donate it,' Seymour held out his hand, 'to the first worthy charity.'

'Just what I had in mind,' Compo re-pocketed the notes and signalled for them to empty their glasses.

A 1958 Bentley turned into the gatepost. There was a thump no louder than the closing of a door.

68

'An old Bently,' Clegg said, 'has just turned into the gate.'

The announcement produced no reaction from the other two who were engaged in a quarrel over the Armpit Millionaire's money.

'Not into the gateway,' Clegg elaborated. 'The gate.'

This time they looked and saw Captain Cosgrave walk to the front of his car, wearing an expression of profound confusion.

Seymour's social geiger counter began clicking madly. 'It's Cosgrave from the Hall.' Abandoning his glass he rose to his feet. 'It's times like this a chap needs the comfort of his own kind.'

They watched him trek rapidly across the car park, his smile of greeting so broad they could see it from behind.

'A spot of bother, Captain?'

'I am gravely disappointed,' Cosgrave confessed, 'with the behaviour of this impulsive gatepost.'

'Buckled your wing a smidgin,' Seymour inspected the damage. 'Lucky I came along. I have a brother-in-law, a wizard in these matters.'

'Must be useful that,' Cosgrave eyed Seymour enviously. 'My brother-in-law's in the Foreign Office. And I needn't tell you of what small utility they've always been.'

'If you'd care to reverse her a yard or two, Captain, I'll guide you in.'

'Good man,' Cosgrave's attention was focusing with some surprise on a point behind Seymour. Seymour was embarrassed to see Compo approaching. He began making signals for Compo's withdrawal which Compo read correctly but cheerfully ignored. He chuckled at the condition of the Bentley's front wing.

'Hey up! Tha's made a right old cock-up there then.'

Seymour closed his eyes as if in pain.

Cosgrave's mouth hung open as he continued to stare at the grinning Compo. 'Incredible,' he managed to stammer.

'I can explain this,' Seymour began.

'Uncanny how much he resembles my mother.' He took a closer look. 'Astonishing. It's not so much the face. It's the general shape. And the way they dress particularly. They must use the same tailor.'

He got back in his car leaving Compo frowning.

'What's he on about?'

'He thinks you look like Lady Georgina,' Clegg said.

'Cheeky twonk,' Compo glared at the Bentley. Seymour's cane was waving busily as he supervised the withdrawal from the gatepost.

'Lady Georgina,' Compo sniffed. 'Was that the old party in wellies and a tatty hat what was doing the gardening at the Hall? She looked terrible.'

'Not everybody,' Clegg placed a congratulatory hand on Compo, 'gets mistaken for an aristocrat.'

A toothy offending squeal of wounded Bentley marked a successful exit from the stonework. Seymour, not without some danger to himself, got the Captain parked. They watched Cosgrave concentrating fiercely as he tried to lock his car. Alignment of key with keyhole seemed to be the difficulty.

'Allow me,' Seymour was in high good humour at all this rubbing shoulders with the gentry. He locked the car and re-offered its owner the key.

'I wish,' the Captain swayed with the fervour of his admiration, 'I could do that. Did you see that?' He invited Clegg to share his admiration. Then again he was staring at Compo. 'Mother?' he enquired.

'He's stoned out of his brain,' Compo pronounced and found himself jerked to one side by the horrified Seymour.

'Do you mind! I'm establishing a good rapport here.'

'Excuse me,' came Clegg's rather anxious tones. 'Could you both pop back for a minute?'

They looked and saw him struggling to support the weight of the Captain who had discovered an exceptional gift for collapsing to the floor. It was a talent which, judging by his expression, was as much of a surprise to himself as it was to Clegg. They went to Clegg's aid and propped Cosgrave against his Bentley.

'My damn legs,' he offered in apology. 'Running amok. I can't understand it. They've always been so reliable.'

70

Compo was in range now of the Captain's whisky breath. 'Tha's thoroughly puddled, owd love.'

Seymour groaned.

The Captain clutched Compo, fiercely grateful. 'My God! I hope that's it.' His mood lightened briefly. 'It could be. It's been an emotional day. I've downed a few.' He uttered the bleakest sigh. 'I have to get married.'

'What's he whispering?' Seymour asked.

'He's pregnant,' Compo said.

They assisted the Captain to their table. He insisted on buying a round.

'Some people,' Clegg cautioned, 'on such scanty evidence as that he keeps falling down, would be of the opinion that he's had enough.'

'It's allus been a practice of mine,' Compo lied cheerfully as he went for the drinks, 'never to interfere with the whims of the gentry.'

'Besides which, he's in good hands now.' Seymour was passing his hat before the Captain's face which had developed a glazed look. 'Safe hands. We shall return him to the arms of his loved ones.'

'I'm not going near Her-with-the-Wellies.' Clegg was adamant.

The clink of Compo's return revived the Captain in awareness if not in mood.

'Which of you are married?' he enquired in search of advice. 'None?' He couldn't believe it. 'You crafty swine.'

'Hang about,' Compo said. 'We've served our time. Mine ran off wi' a bloke of Polish extraction. His,' he pointed to Clegg, 'died.'

'I've always felt guilty,' Clegg sighed. 'I don't know why. I was never nasty with her. There's just a nagging fear that I might have bored her to death.'

'And his,' Compo chuckled at Seymour, 'took off and got a divorce. Well you would, wouldn't you?'

'Sometimes,' Seymour explained to Cosgrave, 'they can't stand the intellectual heat.'

'So there are ways out?' Cosgrave grasped at the straws of relief.

71

'If tha feels like that about her already,' Compo advised, 'I should scratch her.'

'Trouble is,' the Captain sighed. 'I don't as yet know her. We haven't met thus far.'

'A marriage of convenience,' Seymour explained. 'The aristocracy. They're always at it.'

'Not so damned convenient for me,' the Captain stared at his empty glass. 'I have a most satisfactory relationship with the barmaid here.'

'Ruby?' Compo pricked up his ears.

'Ruby,' the Captain nodded.

'Nice little lass is Ruby,' Compo confirmed.

'Only thing that keeps me sober.'

Clegg gasped audibly at this.

'Today, sir,' Cosgrave explained, 'is the day I have to inform her that I have to get married.'

'Another whisky, Captain?' the chastened Clegg suggested. 'You're a gentleman, sir, with an understanding heart.'

The other round before them, Compo was delving into Ruby's genealogy. 'She was an Edwards from Lower Stackpool Street. She married that bad beggar from Barnsley. Turfed her out for some eighteen-year-old informaniac.'

'Excessive lust for information. I like it,' Clegg said.

'Ruby's back now living with her mother.'

'Divorced now,' Cosgrave confirmed.

'Why dunt tha marry Ruby?' Compo asked.

Seymour choked on his drink. 'Please overlook the bald unsophistication of my casual labourer.'

'Bald?' Compo was indignant. 'Who's he calling bald?'

'You don't object then to "casual labourer"?' Clegg was interested sociologically.

'Hell no,' Compo sneered. 'I've allus been casual about labour.'

'The aristocracy,' Seymour smiled ingratiatingly at the gloomy Captain, 'don't marry barmaids.'

72

'Love to marry her,' the Captain sighed. 'Can't afford her. The ancestral home's falling to pieces. It becomes my sad duty to find some wench with a face like a horse who can inject some money into it.' He drank despairingly.

'We share the same problem,' Seymour sympathised. 'I understand, Captain. I too have been undercapitalised and have searched in vain for the right little woman. Someone who could love, cherish and write cheques for me. Not that one wants to get married.'

'I know what you mean,' said the Captain.

'But my genius goes unrecognised for the lack of development money. I'm an inventor, Captain. Dereliction of duty for me to remain, however happily, a bachelor.'

'Exactly.'

'How can I act selfishly when the world needs me?'

'Tha usually manages,' Compo nudged Clegg. 'Dunt he usually manage to act selfishly?'

'Extremely well.'

'Will you be quiet,' Seymour ordered. 'How can you joke when marriage beckons? Do you think it's a step one takes lightly? No.' He shuddered. 'Invention, unhappily, is the mother of necessity.'

They watched Seymour and Cosgrave clink glasses in a despondent toast.

Marina was cycling to her rendezvous. Headscarf tied under her chin, legs in the patterned tights conspicuously flying. She was thinking. What kind of transport can he have got which accommodates a lady's bicycle? The possibilities were sinful.

There was no sign of Howard at the crossroads. She was deliberately early in order to stage-manage his first glimpse of her. She leaned her bicycle against the signpost, wobbling uneasily on high heels in the grass.

How uncharacteristically reckless of him to suggest a meeting in the not yet darkness. Even out here. Alone on a hillside, her knees weak from the pull up the incline.

Vulnerable, she suddenly realised. A helpless, attractive female. At the mercy of any passing male motorist. She retouched her lipstick.

She saw the ambulance approaching. It couldn't be an emergency. Not at that speed. There was something unprofessional about its jerky progress. Could there be some human drama being enacted in there? Some poor soul in the throes of an attack? The driver?

It was tatty for an ambulance. Someone was waving at her. There was smoke coming from its chimney. A chimney? They're using open fires now? My God! They are cutting back in the Health Service! It drew alongside and stopped over abruptly. She could hear patients and bedpans falling in the rear. Howard was smiling down at her.

'Howard!'

'Marina.'

'My God, Howard! I think I just heard a body falling in your ambulance.'

He climbed out in a white coat. A doctor! Her heart leaped proudly. Maybe he's done it through the Open University. He reached to embrace her. She hugged him tightly.

'Oh, Howard! How long have you been qualified?'

His muffled voice from her bosom began to explain.

In a quiet corner of the Best Room at the Seven Shepherds Ruby was feeding coffee to Captain Cosgrave, her pleasant face screwed into a frown of concern.

'How did you get him in this condition?'

'Hey up,' Compo protested. 'He came in this condition.'

'I don't see how he ever got through the gate,' Ruby dabbed the Captain's lips with her own wisp of handkerchief.

'Funny you should say that,' Clegg said.

Ruby groaned. 'Has he dinted the Bentley?'

'My brother-in-law,' Seymour soothed, 'is a dint remover of uncommon skill.'

'You can leave the Captain here,' Ruby said firmly. 'I'll

drive him home.' She glanced professionally at the others. 'You lot look as if you've had a skinful yourselves.'

It came to them with the force of revelation. They went to walk it off.

'Forceful little lady,' Seymour remarked as they climbed the hill behind the Seven Shepherds. 'I hope we've left my friend the Captain in good hands.'

'She's a good lass is Ruby,' Compo affirmed. 'I've seen her blister the paint off big men.'

They paused for breath. Lights were appearing in the distant town. The sun was a red balloon. The Peacock Snatch Squad deep in their bowels began to feel the moths of uncertainty fluttering.

'Ruby!' the Captain exclaimed.

'Welcome back,' Ruby scowled. 'I've been here some time.'

'Are we alone?' He was blinking owlishly.

'Put your glasses on.' She withdrew them from his inside pocket. 'You don't have to pretend with me.'

With the aid of the lenses he was able to see that he was in the Best Room. A pair of unmarrieds were engrossed in each other in the far corner.

'Are they the lot?'

'That's it,' Ruby confirmed. 'One pina collada and a lager and lime.'

She looked delicious. Her small, slim frame in a plain summer dress. No barmaid accessories. No gold jangling at her wrist. No rings as big as marbles. Small pins merely in the pink of her ears. Blonde hair neatly set. Her make-up restrained. Regarding him steadily from shrewd, blue eyes alight with criticism and concern.

'I need a rich wife, Ruby.'

She nodded. 'So you keep telling me.'

75

'It's expected of me. In return for money I can offer a certain breeding.'

'Even your seed,' she went back to the bar, 'is going to be over the limit.'

'He's coming,' Compo reported. They saw the chip van approaching on sidelights. They winced as it swung into the gate but there was no scrape. 'Hey up, he's improving!'

'I'm glad about that,' Clegg said fervently.

They went out to the van. And so did two other couples who were leaving the bar.

'Fish and two chips four times,' one of the men said.

'I'm afraid we're closed this evening for a private party,' Seymour smiled.

'Hang on a minute,' Howard said. 'There's no sense in losing a good order like that.' He turned on his burners again and opened up.

They paced the car park frustratedly watching Howard and Marina doing steady business with customers leaving the pub.

'Money grabber,' Compo said.

It was hot in the van. The fryers were still sizzling as they rode towards 'Harbour Lights' and their appointment with the peacock. They were crammed in the back with Marina's bike, sweating and trying to keep their tender parts from contact with the hot pans. Marina and Howard were holding hands in the front. They swayed round another bend.

'Tell him to keep his hands on the wheel,' Compo protested.

'Amazing how much confidence he's gained in a single evening,' Clegg mopped his face.

'Where's the silencer?' Seymour experienced a moment of planner's panic. 'Who's got the silencer?'

76

'It's here,' Compo snarled, contorting painfully as he struggled to free it. 'Halfway up my—' The van rattled noisily over a pothole obscuring forever the precise anatomical details of the silencer's whereabouts.

They guided Howard into the lay-by near the little river. They got jammed in the doorway in their eagerness to get outside. Howard switched off his lights. It was almost dark. The three recent rear passengers were tottering in the roadway, fanning their faces and gulping the mild evening air. The scents of woodland and vegetation were beginning to collide with the overriding smell of chips. Faint sounds of revelry were coming from the house. Music and laughter.

'He's having a party.'

'Excellent,' Seymour approved. 'It will cover our small noises.'

They jumped as behind them Howard blew the chip van horn.

'I say,' Howard enquired plaintively. 'How long do you think you'll be away?'

'Dammit, Howard,' Seymour raged in suppressed and guilty fury. 'Will you keep your hand off that thing.'

Marina giggled.

'I'm sorry I'm sure,' Howard sulked.

'And open up the side shutters. It's like an oven in there. Get the thing cooled down before it's full of peacock.'

While the sulky Howard opened up, Seymour sent Compo on to the roof to pass down the ladder.

'And watch what you're doing up there,' Howard cautioned proprietorially. 'I don't want it scratching.'

'You're really getting the hang of the self-employment, Howard,' Clegg said. 'Your first day and it's changed your whole personality.'

'Aagh!' Compo yelped. Seymour dropped the silencer.

'Now what?'

'This friggin chimney's hot.'

'Lady's present,' Howard said.

'All of you keep quiet,' Seymour retrieved the silencer and listened anxiously for sounds of alarm.

77

'How's he expect any beggar to blister silently?' Compo was blowing on his hands.

They lowered the ladder with Howard fussing parentally all the time.

'Will you get out from underfoot?' Seymour hissed. 'I hate treading on chip-van proprietors.'

Compo climbed down. They carried the ladder to the river bank and paused to listen. The noises from the house remained friendly. They found a place where the banks were shallowest and crabbed their way down to the water's edge. In the almost dark at ankle height were occasional clouds of mist. The river gurgled merrily. It's laughing at us, Clegg decided, and who can blame it? It was blacker than its surroundings except where eddies churned in muted sparkle. They could smell the water.

Seymour adjusted the silencer under his arm. 'Right,' he whispered to Compo. 'Off you go across.'

'Hey up!' Compo objected in a far from whisper which sent Seymour hissing for quiet. 'Why me?'

'You're the one in the wellies.'

'That'll be useful,' Compo snorted. 'If it's six foot deep.'

'These little hill-country rivers are never deep,' Seymour scoffed. 'You see fishermen wading them all the time.'

'With wellies up to here,' Compo said making a gesture not entirely lost in the dark.

'It's your big birthday idea,' Seymour snarled. 'Somebody has to take one end of the ladder across. And I'm carrying the silencer.'

'In case anybody happened to be looking at me,' Clegg's voice came from the dark, 'I think it's only fair to warn you that I'm a natural back-up man. It would be completely out of character for me to start being pushy about going first.'

'Stuff me,' Compo sighed as he accepted the inevitable. 'What a pair of big girls to come moonlighting with.'

'Just feel your way carefully,' Seymour advised. 'You'll have the ladder to hang on to and we'll be holding it.'

'Tha better be,' Compo threatened. 'Because if tha lets me take all the weight before I get across I'll come back and stuff it up thee—'

78

'There is no need,' Seymour interrupted hastily, 'to take that attitude. We're all here helping you, aren't we?'

'To get wet.'

Compo lowered an exploratory boot into the water. He found firm bottom with scarcely half his welly wet. The little river was suddenly muscular. He could feel it tugging at his foot. All of a sudden he admits it's my idea. He stepped in with the other foot. Comes to risking a ducking and he can't wait to give me all the credit. Pebbles were shifting under his feet.

He turned in the water and took a grip on the end of the ladder.

'Now don't start shoving it out,' he warned. 'Just remember I'm on the end of this. Just feed it out gently when tha feels me pulling it.'

'What a production he makes of things,' Seymour whispered to Clegg. 'You'd think he was crossing Niagara.'

They could see in the starlight the dark shape of Compo feeling his way backwards ultra cautiously. They could feel his weight on the ladder.

Clegg began singing softly.

'Happy birthday to you.'

'Bog off!' the shape said.

Up on the road Howard embraced Marina. It was comfortable for neither since she was eating chips from a paper.

'What are they doing crossing rivers in the dark?'

'It's yet another example,' Howard was almost intoxicated by the provocative mix of perfume and vinegar, 'of what men will do for desire of a woman.'

'What kind of women are they hoping to find in them trees at this time of night?'

'Not women, love. Peacocks.'

She paused in mid chip. 'Sounds more like an example then of what men will do for desire of a peacock.'

'They're doing it for Nora.' Howard explained the birthday plan.

79

'I think that's lovely.' Marina was impressed. 'I think that's the sweetest thing I've ever heard.'

'No more than other men have done, my love,' Howard said plaintively. 'Who have gone to the limits of devotion with a chip van.'

'We've got to help them,' Marina removed her high heels.

'We are helping,' Howard protested. 'I'm stuck out here miles from anywhere missing the late-night pub trade.'

But Marina was gone, wincing across road grit in stocking feet to the soft relief of the grass. She could hear them faintly. One hand clutching her chips she felt her way silently down the bank.

Compo's weight on the ladder was growing as he crossed. Clegg and Seymour were straining to keep it steady.

'Don't just hang on it,' Seymour hissed. 'You're supposed to be carrying it.'

'Shurrup! It's getting deeper here.'

All progress stopped while Compo explored with his toe for a suddenly elusive bottom. He swore as water filled one of his wellies.

'Language!' Seymour said and winced as he got a lot more by return of service.

'Just hold the fizzin ladder still,' Compo snorted.

I could be in bed, Clegg was thinking. He was aware that to most people his old-fashioned bedroom with its wallpaper hung by the dead would appear unenticing but to him it was beginning to look better by the minute. The dark looked better from a bedroom. It was so much bigger out here. Images from horror movies were arriving unbidden. Don't be stupid he told himself. The only thing you have to fear out here is these other crackpots you're with.

A hand tapped his shoulder from behind. He whinnied in fear and let go the ladder. Compo's startled answering yelp was cut short by a splash.

'Sorry,' Marina whispered. 'I was wondering if anyone fancied a chip.'

There came from the river a series of four-letter splutters.

'Lady's present,' Howard winced, from somewhere up the road.

'Will you all keep quiet,' the agitated Seymour hissed.

It had the effect of stifling conversation in the dry but the sounds of seals disporting continued unabated. They backed in primitive fear away from the shape which rose from the river and came squelching soggily ashore. It was muttering fiercely.

'Oh stop fussing,' Seymour ordered. 'The mood you're in you'll soon dry.' He backed hastily from the threatened attack, his silencer raised like a cross to ward off vampires.

'Did you fall in, love?' Marina enquired.

'Fall in? Fall in?' Compo spat mud with all the venom of a small, aquatic dragon. 'I was friggin' pushed. Stabbed in mid-stream with a freakin' ladder.'

'Not guilty,' Clegg said. 'I was stifling a scream at the time.'

'What I fail to understand,' Seymour announced, 'is why you came back this side. Why didn't you exploit the situation and take the ladder across since you were all wet anyway?'

He scrambled up the bank with a soggy fury at his heels. Then all froze at the sound of voices, across the river, in the trees.

A torch was waving. Two men in party clothes with drinks in hand were wending an obviously unfamiliar path towards the river. They paused.

'Here,' one said. 'It's strong again here.'

They were sniffing the air. The scent led them to the bank.

'It's over there,' one said. 'Fish and chips. I'm telling you.'

'What would fish and chips be doing out here?'

'I don't know but I could murder a good few.'

'Couldn't we all?' the other one said with feeling. 'Anything but that hamburger crap he's serving.'

'Calls it a barbecue. There are people back there starving.'

'I'd give two quid for a plastic trayful.'

'How do we get across the fizzin' river?'

'Don't bother,' Compo shouted, splashing back into the water with the ladder. 'We'll deliver.'

* * *

81

The music was pounding. Guests were dancing on the lawns of 'Harbour Lights'. The Armpit Millionaire wearing a chef's hat and a frilly pink shirt was wielding a long spatula in his purpose-built barbecue area. With the same care for a lost ball that he brought to his game of golf he was shepherding the sizzling discs he had bought sensationally cheaply because their safety date was exceeded. The bread buns were yesterday's and therefore again represented exceptional value.

It enables me, he glanced with pride at the number of his guests, to offer hospitality on a lavish scale. Me mam would have been proud.

He saw his wife in a glittering sheath of a dress pass into shadow from floodlight. His heart swelled large in the barbecue area. She was enfolded closely, as they danced, in the arms of a grey-haired smoothie whose hand was on her bottom. She is being groped, the Armpit Millionaire noted with approval, by a chairman of three companies. We've certainly come a long way.

In the undergrowth at the woodland fringes bordering the lawns the small nocturnal wildlife was enjoying hospitality on a lavish scale where party guests had jettisoned the unacceptable face of their beefburgers. Mysterious odours had led guests towards other guests concealed in the trees as they wolfed surreptitiously. A busy shuttle service had grown between the house and the secret source of fish and chips.

Howard and Marina were going flat out in the van. Great! Howard mopped a steaming brow. Alone with the lady of your choice in the absence of your wife and we might as well be chained to the oars of a Roman galley. Still – he ran his fingers through the pound coins in the tin – virtue is its own reward.

Another damn great moth! Marina gathered a scoopful of chips and winced. I hate big fluttery things – this one for instance. She groaned as Seymour came briskly from darkness with his order book full.

Down the river Compo and Clegg were ferrying chips across the ladder and returning with money and orders to come. It was two pounds a throw.

82

'On account of the danger,' Compo challenged any protesting client and there were few. He was still squelching a bit, adding a soggy lustre to his argument.

'Look at the poor old man,' a woman chided her financially timid husband. 'He's somebody's grandad wringing wet through. Get him paid and stop embarrassing me.'

'Poor old man?' Compo snorted to a grinning Clegg. I'll give her poor old man before the night's out. He marked her in somebody's torchlight for attention later.

'Oh heck!' Clegg sighed. 'Life was simpler when all you used to pinch were a few pheasants.'

'I should never sleep,' Compo shuddered, 'if I let her go home wi' that impression. It's such a slur on me macho image.' He raised his voice. 'And no change given,' he growled at the woman's husband in the tones of a commando leader ordering 'no prisoners'. Ruining that worthy's evening completely as he watched his fiver speeding across the river in return for fish and chips twice. He turned on his wife.

'Listen,' he said in a broken voice. 'I bought you that scrabble board. Why don't we stay home more at nights?'

'You can't even spell,' she snapped. 'All you can do is count.'

Clegg overburdened chipwise was no Nureyev on the ladder. I've had better nightmares he decided, retrieving a boot from the water. Yorkshire waiter by moonlight. You can keep it. It was a race to wobble across before the heat of his cargo could pass in unbalancing thermals through his jacket and waistcoat, cardigan, shirt and vest. He could feel it coming. It would be summer! When I'm frolicking about here half-undressed. With a sigh of relief he dispensed his bounty on the farther shore. And this is only the beginning. We've still got a peacock to insert in a drainpipe.

It's been a success, the Armpit Millionaire decided, resting from his culinary labours with a large brandy and an even larger lady (in places anyway) who modelled occasionally for

83

a manufacturer of ladies' outsize wear. People look contented. Well fed. Plastered. He frowned and made signs to the barman who signalled back that yes he was now serving the watered stuff.

'We felt we'd just scream if it was Ibiza again,' the outsize model said. 'The night life can really be tacky.' A head taller than him, she tossed back her glossy dark hair. 'I like,' she looked at him challengingly, 'intelligent men. Idiots bore me.'

'I saw you in that corset advert,' he said. 'I clipped it out. It's in me wallet. I've never seen anybody look better in a corset. I asked Harry to bring you. He owes me a favour. You look terrific,' his voice was husky. 'Sideways.'

How intelligent! she was thinking. They went into the house.

They were wiping down at the van. The last customers gone. They stepped out for a breather. Behind them the ticking of the cooling pans. Howard leaned weakly against the van. I had no idea, he was thinking, how exhausting a bit of hanky panky is. People have entirely the wrong impression. He fanned a little night air around his sticky shirt. He was reviewing his concept of fidelity. It was awash with a more attractive light. Staying home might not be all that exciting but by God it was easier.

He glanced sideways at Marina who was repairing her face in the door mirror by torchlight, her nerves strung taut for the first dive of insect aerobatics.

She's very attractive from this angle in door mirrors, Howard admitted. She can send your senses reeling. I just hope she's not anticipating anything physical. I'm as passionate as the next man but its getting late. Pearl would understand. Pearl always understands when I've got a headache.

* * *

84

'I telled thee,' Compo cackled triumphantly. 'I telled thee we'd find it roosting in a tree.'

'Switch that damned light off,' Seymour hissed. 'We don't want to get caught now.'

They listened in the moonlight. Music was pounding from the house. Seymour had the silencer.

'I brought this.' Clegg unfurled it from his pocket. 'It's a dog lead and collar. It was in our wash house. I don't know how long it's been there.'

Compo was hugely amused. 'Tha dunt think tha's going to walk it on a collar and lead.' He fell about.

'I'm unfamiliar,' Clegg admitted, 'with the practices of peacocks.'

'You did your best,' Seymour condescended. 'Right. Here's the plan.'

'Ooh, a plan!' Compo mimed being impressed. 'We don't just snatch a peacock. We have a plan.'

He was thumped with the silencer and hauled to his place in Seymour's tight conspiratorial circle. 'Stage One. While I dazzle the creature with the light – you two climb the tree and bring it down.'

Clegg left the little circle. 'I don't like it already.'

'Dammit, it's not as if it's high,' Seymour protested. 'If we had a stool you could reach it.'

'It's big.' Clegg snatched the torch and played it on the peacock. It was perched near the end of a low branch a few feet above their heads. It regarded them warily. 'Look at the size of it! That's not some canary.'

'Let's not use the torch unnecessarily,' Seymour warned. They went back to moonlight. The bird murmured. They tensed, fearing the ear-splitting squawk.

'You've upset it,' Seymour hissed.

'Not half as much as it's upsetting me,' Clegg hissed back. The bird settled again.

'It wants to be big,' Compo said. 'I'm not turning up for Nora's birthday wi' some midget peacock.'

'Did you bring the ladder?' Seymour sighed. 'Did nobody think to bring the ladder?'

85

'Including you,' the undeceived Compo said.

'I was carrying the silencer. Am I expected to think of everything?'

They propped the ladder against the peacock's branch. It offered no objection.

'Up you go then,' Seymour encouraged. There remained an absence of productive movement. 'What's the matter with you?'

'Clegg's right. It is big. Looks like a chuffin' Lancaster bomber from here.'

'Oh very well. Hold this.' Seymour thrust the silencer into Clegg's hands. 'Do it yourself, Seymour.' He removed his jacket. He paused with a foot on the ladder. 'When I give the signal, you will dazzle the bird with the light. I shall throw my jacket over its head. It will then remain perfectly still.'

I love his positive thinking, Clegg decided.

'You may then turn out the light. Join me on the ladder and together we shall lift the bird down.' Seymour took hold of the ladder. 'Any questions?'

'Point of order,' Clegg said. 'Do they bite?'

Seymour stepped back from the ladder.

They were changing records at the party. It seemed unnaturally quiet. A breeze was ruffling the tops of the trees. The moon was waiting for their next move. The amplified music began throbbing again.

'No,' scoffed Seymour, making no move back to the ladder. 'Why should they bite?'

'I just thought it was a possibility that might occur to it,' Clegg said, 'when it realised some muffin was about to bury it in a jacket.'

'Beats trousers,' Compo plucked at his own pair which were still adhesively damp. 'Especially mine.'

'Amen to that,' Clegg agreed.

'Anyway, how big a bite could it be?' Seymour laughed less

than convincingly. 'When's the last time you heard of a man-eating peacock? What we have here is simply an outsize chicken.'

'That makes two of us,' Clegg admitted.

'However,' Seymour continued, 'in order to observe every precaution, why don't I hold the torch to be ready instantly for any signs of aggression?'

'Three of us,' Clegg amended.

'Oh give us thee jacket!' Compo snatched the garment from Seymour's grasp and approached the ladder. They shone the light. They watched him climb. 'How do bird,' he said. He reached towards it. They winced at the squawk. It came from Compo. He came fast down the ladder, sucking his finger. 'It does,' he announced. 'It bites.'

'Happy birthday to you,' Clegg sang softly.

'Bog off!' the intrepid birdman said.

'We're going to have to take it by surprise.' Seymour explained a change of tactics. 'The ladder's too slow. It can see us coming.'

'Us?' Compo snorted. 'I didn't notice any overcrowding on that ladder.'

'You'll be going up much quicker next time,' Seymour promised.

'How come it's my turn again?'

'It knows you now,' Clegg said and ducked a swipe from Compo's wet hat.

'You'll be travelling far too fast for it this time.' Seymour led them directly underneath the branch. 'We'll stand here quietly for a moment till it gets used to us. Then when I give the signal, Clegg and I will hoist you up. You'll be going like a rocket. You drop the jacket over it. Bingo!' Seymour at least seemed optimistic. 'You bring the bird back with you on the way down.'

If he expected applause there came none. Above them the bird clucked uneasily.

'It seems to me,' Compo said finally, 'to be full of what tha might call snags.'

'Good heavens, man! We're going to be here all night if you

87

can't develop a more positive attitude. Actually you've got the easy part. We're doing the lifting.'

Compo remained unimpressed. 'Hey up, Norm!' He turned to Clegg. 'Does it seem reasonable to thee?'

'Absolutely,' Clegg sighed. 'I hate lying to you but this is an emergency.' He patted a stubbly cheek by moonlight. 'You'll be doing it for Nora.'

'I'll do it for Nora,' Compo agreed, settling his hat on more firmly. He accepted the jacket. They bent and seized him by welly and thigh.

'Are you ready?' Seymour enquired.

'I'm ready. I'm ready.'

Grunting and straining they launched him for the sky and heard a chunky sound which proved to be his head in contact with the branch.

'You great, steaming dozy pair o' buttocks!'

It seemed like a good time for abandoning Plan Two. They released him hastily and withdrew.

'I like the casual way,' Seymour sniffed haughtily, 'he just calmly drops a person's jacket on the floor.'

The peacock flapped lazily to the ground. It clucked a few times and began to strut towards the house.

'We've got it now,' Seymour said.

They stalked it through the trees, losing it frequently in shadows and reluctant to risk their light so close to the house. They had ample cover, at least, for the noise they were making. All was absorbed in the pounding music.

'Excellent,' Seymour pronounced. 'Ideal conditions. If it does squawk a bit now – who's going to hear it?' He began calling seductively to the bird. 'Here chuck chuck chuck.'

'Just look at him!' Compo scoffed. 'Colonel fizzin' Sanders.'

Seymour was advancing by moonlight. A matador with his jacket outstretched, leaving Clegg holding the silencer. Life, Clegg was thinking, offers infinite possibilities. Here I am

88

standing on the fringe of a barbecue holding a drainpipe.

Seymour dived for the bird's head and got his jacket entangled in shrubbery. The peacock flapped ponderously into the tree.

'I'm not playing rockets again. Forget it. Don't even mention it.'

'Oh stop going on so,' Seymour was brushing his jacket. 'Nobody asked you. We shall try,' he announced, 'my other idea.' He became all charm and good fellowship. 'Norman,' he said, slipping an arm round Clegg.

'No,' said Clegg.

'You haven't heard it yet.'

'I don't care.' Clegg was backing away. Compo was cackling with evil glee.

'It's simplicity itself, this time,' Seymour seized Clegg by the drainpipe. 'The bird's near the trunk this time. We just lean against the tree. You stand on my shoulders and—'

They grabbed Clegg before he could flee.

'Bingo!'

'Bingo?' Clegg whimpered. 'Don't say that word. You said it to him and he got hit with a tree.'

'Tha'll be all right, Norm,' Compo chuckled as they led Clegg towards the tree. 'Would we let thee do it if it weren't a good idea?'

'I have to tell you,' Clegg said, 'your personality is a lot less attractive since that bang on the head.'

'Take your boots off,' Seymour ordered.

They were at the very fringes of the trees. They could see floodlight through shrubbery. As he tussled with his laces, Clegg could hear laughter. Untroubled voices. Life goes on normally, he sighed, just a few yards away.

He gave Compo his boots. 'If I don't come back,' he said solemnly. 'They're yours.'

'Ta,' Compo said.

'You'll need these,' Seymour handed him jacket and silencer. 'When you get up there, you'll be the man on the spot.'

He's not kidding, Clegg thought.

89

'Use your own discretion whether to get its head in the jacket or straight into the silencer.'

'I can't balance with me hands full of these.'

What a night it's becoming for frivolous objection, Seymour concluded. They have no consideration for the executive stress involved in pushing these matters through. 'Very well, wear the jacket. Put it on over your own. You can take it off if you need it when you get up there.'

They assisted Clegg into Seymour's jacket. It came nearly down to his knees. The sleeves drooped brokenly beyond the extent of his fingers. Seymour fastened both jackets and tucked the silencer inside. The curved end protruded under Clegg's nose, the other end hung like a third leg. They walked him stiffly to the base of the tree.

Seymour hugged the trunk and bent down. Compo was much impressed by Clegg's appearance now.

'Tha looks,' he struggled to suppress his giggles, 'just like one of that mob what used to work for Snow White.'

'Give him a leg up,' Seymour hissed. He yelped as he got his back scraped by the drainpipe. Clegg was ordered sharply to raise his periscope.

He was wobbling on Seymour's shoulders, clutching the tree and very aware that he was being raised with much moaning and grunting nearer to the bird. He daren't look. He kept his eyes buried in his forearms as his hands slowly climbed the trunk.

'Stand still,' Seymour gasped. 'Don't shuffle about.'

Clegg, at their maximum height now, was embracing the tree with a death lock.

'Can you reach the bird?' Seymour panted.

'It's slightly to thee left,' Compo advised.

Oh God, Clegg groaned. What does he mean – 'slightly'? How far is slightly? It was damned uncomfortable embracing a tree with a drainpipe down your waistcoat.

'Can you reach it?' Seymour insisted.

'Let's look at it the other way,' Clegg said. 'Can it reach me? What's it doing?'

'Oh for goodness sake tell him what it's doing,' Seymour

90

grunted, his own vision somewhat restricted by the closeness of the tree.

'It's not doing a lot of anything,' Compo reported. 'It's just sitting there. Does tha want me to poke it?'

'No!' Clegg responded with alarm.

'Keep still,' Seymour groaned. 'I wish you'd stop leaping about on people's shoulders. Now pay attention. We're going to turn now.'

'Oh hell,' Clegg moaned.

'Until we've got our right shoulders leaning against the tree. Then you'll have both hands free.'

Great! Clegg decided. Just what you need when you don't like heights. Both hands free.

Seymour grunted with strain as he began the movement. Clegg steered his face round the drainpipe and laid his right cheek against the bark. He began to draw in his right shoulder like a tortoise pulling in its head. Both he and Seymour were now leaning against the tree.

Clegg shifted the silencer to a more comfortable position and tried to peek through his fingers at the bird but couldn't even find his fingers which were hidden somewhere in Seymour's sleeves.

'Have you never seen,' a boozy male, voice enquired, 'the Moonlight Orchid?'

'If you're lying to me, Edgar,' a penetrating female voice said, 'I shall be furious.'

They were startlingly near and coming closer. Compo ducked behind a bush. Clegg and Seymour had no alternative but to freeze where they were.

'I have too much respect for you, Mrs Danbury,' the drunk said with boozy solemnity, 'ever to lie.'

'Don't paw me, Edgar. If you're going to paw me I'm going back now.'

They had slowed to argue. 'None of your friends in the city,' Edgar told her, 'will ever have seen the Moonlight Orchid. It blooms only briefly.'

'Is it far?'

'Botanists,' Edgar affirmed with grave dignity, 'would

91

travel to China for a glimpse of the Moonlight Orchid.'

'You're in no condition for travelling to China.'

Seymour's Clegg-laden shoulders were hurting. He gritted his teeth.

'It is the Taj Mahal of flowers.'

'Will there be nettles?' Mrs Danbury asked.

'And should it not be in bloom, why then,' Edgar embraced her clumsily, 'we shall be together and wait.'

'Will you stop it, Edgar!'

'I love you, Mrs Danbury.' He saw her face forming the scream before it ripped shatteringly past his ears. She was gaping pop-eyed at the creature. Ten-foot tall and leaning furtively against the tree. She saw its handless arms waving. And God knows what appalling thing protruding from its clothing. She screamed again, recovered the use of ice-cold limbs and fled towards the house with Edgar blundering after.

'Not so loud, Mrs Danbury! Was it something I said?'

Seymour's knees were giving way. Clegg wailed as he felt himself falling. The peacock bored by all the noise and uncharmed by the waving sleeves now falling past its face, flapped irritably towards the ground to land on Compo who was rising from his bush. Both squawked in alarm.

'He's got it,' Seymour announced.

'Get it off!' Compo demanded.

'Don't be a fool, man!' Seymour snarled. 'Hang on to it.' Seymour divested the winded Clegg of his outermost jacket. He went to Compo's aid and struggled to quieten the agitated bird.

'Get me out,' Compo appealed through a mouthful of feathers. 'Oh God! It's so dark under here.'

Someone was turning the music down. A group on the lawn had gathered about the hysterical Mrs Danbury. The puzzled Edgar was trying to recruit sympathisers.

'Never touched the woman.' He flinched at the sound of her sobs. 'I may have told her a harmless fiction.'

'It was ghastly,' she sobbed.

'All right,' Edgar protested. 'One hand. May have stumbled inadvertently. One lousy hand.'

92

'There,' she pointed. 'Lurking in the trees. I saw it. Ten-foot tall. With no hands. Just this – giant thing.'

The noise of muffled peacock lent force to her story.

'Listen,' she shrieked. 'It's angry.'

And it was. It was like trying to carry a pillowcase full of cats. They had it tucked under their arms. And they were legging it for the river.

Pearl was waiting for the chip van. She was pacing between her front door and the garden gate. Another five minutes, she decided, and I'll call the police. Suppose he's lying injured. She had a vision of him lying senseless, unnaturally twisted among chips. He's not a gifted driver. Was it too big and clumsy for him? He's not a gifted anything. He needs me behind him. I should have gone with him. You let 'em out your sight for two minutes! If he's dead I'll kill him. She reached for the phone. She dialled nine, nine – and stopped. She put down the phone. She went back outside. On the other hand, did she dare call the police? Suppose he was trapped in a lay-by somewhere with that man-eating Marina. Couldn't get home if he wanted to. She was too big and clumsy for him. You don't want the police charging in on that. There was only one light still burning in the street. The world was in bed. Where was he? Was it accident or adultery? If he's not dead I'll kill him.

She heard the van turning the corner, climbing the hill. From a pack of feelings of relief she selected the card with the fiercest expression with which to greet him. He climbed down from the cab wearily.

'Where the devil have you been?'

'I tried to be earlier,' he rattled his money tin, 'but pressure of events.'

She opened the van rear door and went inside, nose alert for perfume. And it was there, remotely overpowered by the smell of wet clothes and something else. She picked up a feather.

She marched him into the house. She remained unsoftened

93

by his plaintive rattling of the money tin. It's good to be home, he was thinking. It means trouble but there's a real sense of security. He shuddered at the recent memory of the overcrowded rear of his van. A lady's bike, three lunatics and a peacock. Enough for an inexperienced driver to be going on with. Especially when the noises began. He shuddered again. As long as I live, he pleaded secretly, may I never be present a second time when a peacock is being fitted with a silencer.

Pearl closed the kitchen door and turned to face him, arms folded, face grim. 'Now!' she glared accusingly. 'I want to know who you've got that wears perfume, is wet through and covered with feathers.'

He sighed. He looked at her with respect and affection and, in the way of husbands everywhere, began to lie unconvincingly.

Three heads and a drainpipe were peering round a corner in Kelham Street. Except for parked cars the street spread empty under its sodium lights.

'All clear,' Seymour beckoned them onward. Compo had the peacock on the lead. With its head in the drainpipe it was behaving impeccably. It seemed quite happy. They tiptoed across the road quickly and headed for the shadows.

They were making their way by the back streets to Compo's. Rendered somewhat self-conscious by their new companion they were seeking to shun human company. Clegg glanced at the bird as it dipped and rolled beside them, its claws scraping quietly on the pavement, the drainpipe, like a tall chimney, rising and falling. 'I don't know why I couldn't go home with Howard in the van, seeing as I only live next door.'

'And break up a great team?' Seymour shook his head. 'We're in this together. Besides, we didn't know how the peacock was going to behave. We might have needed all hands.'

'He's behaving like a good 'un,' Compo patted the neck

below the drainpipe, 'is Prudence.' From the drainpipe came muffled noises of appreciation.

'Prudence,' Seymour corrected, 'is not a boy's name.'

'If tha'd kept thee big gob shut,' Compo sighed, 'he'd never have known.' He patted the bird again reassuringly. 'We'll call him Pinkerton then. I noticed when we were fitting him for the drainpipe he had little pink eyes.'

'And I noticed he had about thirty-two claws,' Clegg said. 'And what seemed like forty pairs of wings.'

'He's quietened down nicely,' Compo said proudly. 'He's a good lad is Pinkerton.'

'They laughed,' Seymour complained, 'when I invented the peacock silencer. But here it is. Works like a charm. Do I hear applause?'

The night remained silent.

'I hear nothing. Nothing.'

Compo blew a raspberry. Seymour sighed heavily.

'We like your peacock silencer, Seymour, honest,' Clegg said, touched by Seymour's pain.

'Even Pinkerton likes thee silencer,' Compo agreed.

'Oh God,' Clegg groaned. 'Don't say we're going to have as much trouble getting him out as we did getting him in!'

'You see the irony of it,' Seymour raised a critical glance towards the heavens. 'How rarely a thing works first time. Straight from the drawing board. And I, Seymour Utterthwaite, have pulled it off. The inventor's dream.' He stopped and gazed sadly at the bobbing drainpipe as it passed. 'And where's the market for it?' He trudged after them. Pinkerton's tail was trailing. 'Where's the demand? I'm ahead of my time,' he consoled himself. 'That's tomorrow's technology you're towing on a lead there.'

They came to Vincent Street.

In a dark shop doorway at the bottom of Vincent Street, young Byron Pilbeam, his acne throbbing with anticipation, had a pair of night glasses trained on a bedroom window.

95

Beside him the Polaroid Kid was squinting through a zoom telephoto. The light in the bedroom was pink shaded and in this sensuous rosy glow the Polaroid Kid could see, in heart-racing hazy outline which sent him fumbling at his focus, the bulging curves of – a mahogany wardrobe.

'It's a wardrobe,' he glared at Byron.

'I know it's a wardrobe,' Byron explained with a native dignity proper to the possessor of five O levels. 'But there'll be more. I haven't been coming out here for yonks now secret wardrobe peeping.'

'It better be good,' the Polaroid Kid checked the street nervously. He was host to unsettling images of a constabulary task force, trained to emasculate such as he, creeping ever closer, nightscopes steady.

'You've got better things to do?' Byron sneered.

'Than wardrobes,' the Polaroid Kid agreed.

Young Byron Pilbeam raised his U-boat glasses and made a sweep of the target. I should have stayed a lone wolf he decided. This hunting in packs is not for me.

They saw Mister Fothergill pass the window in vest and braces. The Polaroid Kid groaned. He liked it better with just the wardrobe. He lowered his zoom telephoto and checked the street. He saw three dark figures and a Thing melt into the shadows.

Though his mouth was dry and his breathing suddenly laboured it was nerves he decided. Had to be. No way was there any such thing as the Thing he imagined he'd seen stalking weirdly all neck and no— He rubbed his eyes. Too much squinting through lenses at forbidden wardrobes. He giggled nervously. The Thing from Vincent Street.

He was just on the point of sharing the joke with his nearest U-boat commander who, with the dedication to his hazardous trade of that stealthy breed, was still glued to the eyepiece of Herr Zeiss, when the three shapes and the Thing from Vincent Street emerged from behind a parked Toyota. What would have been a cry of fear died from sheer panic in his throat. They were forty yards away and coming nearer, and though as yet no more than silhouettes, it was appallingly

96

clear as its neck bobbed vigorously in the obscene delicacy of its ghastly walk, that the Thing from Vincent Street was without a head.

The Polaroid Kid shrieked and left the doorway like a missile. Compo, Seymour and Clegg collided in startled confusion as they dived for the cover of a parked Capri, hauling Pinkerton with them.

Young Byron Pilbeam, when the shriek went off in his ear, had jarred his eyebrows painfully and decoding this signal from the Polaroid Kid as meaning 'raiders approaching' was already proceeding at all speed to safer waters. He was legging it at a fast, adolescent clip up Vincent Street when his feet became entangled with a drainpipe with a lot of feathers in it.

He managed to glide for ten yards, arms windmilling desperately before he went crashing down, depressing his spirits heavily as he landed smack on his binoculars.

Still at a loss to understand why the quiet street had suddenly erupted with flying feet they remained cowering behind the Capri in case any further bodies were bearing down on them. Pinkerton, equally baffled inside his drainpipe, was wondering what next this night?

Young Byron Pilbeam still fearing the hand of the law on his collar was back in full flight thinking Why pick on me. A young male with a natural interest in sex when the street's full of dirty old men prowling about behind Capris not fooling anybody with that lame pretence of taking their emu for a walk. Go pick on them. Leave those of us with acne alone. I didn't ask to be interested in ladies half-undressed. Computer programming used to be enough. He remembered the three startled faces recently passed. Don't tell me it won't be over even at that age!

'Where did he come from?' Compo soothed the ruffled Pinkerton. 'All legs and binoculars. Charging into people's peacocks.'

Seymour was scanning the street cautiously from the cover of the Capri. 'All clear,' he announced.

'That's what you said before,' the shaken Clegg accused.

97

'And suddenly we're in the flight path of rocket-assisted adolescents.'

'See for yourself,' Seymour invited in suppressed angry whispers. 'I don't know who they were. But they were up to no good. It's quiet again now.'

They resumed their journey.

Upstairs at his window Mister Fothergill gasped. When his wife returned from the bathroom she found him sitting on the bed. His colour drained, his expression ghastly.

'I don't know why you drink the stuff,' she snapped. 'When it makes you feel like that.'

'Don't go near the window, lass,' he said in tones of awful solemnity. 'Whatever you do I want you to promise me you won't look out there.'

'You come home with a skinful. You don't make any sense.'

'Have we got a crucifix?' he asked.

'Silly beggar,' she scolded. He closed his eyes as she went to the window. He heard the sharp and shuddering intake of her breath. They held each other in the rosy light.

'What was it?' she sobbed.

'It was three God knows what kind of creatures,' he patted warm bulges of the cotton nightdress. 'Walking a headless ostrich.'

They closed the curtains.

'P.C. Two Four Nine,' his personal radio crackled. He unclipped it from his tunic.

'P.C. Two Four Nine. Over.'

'Disturbance Vincent Street,' the electronic voice wavered through noises like bacon frying. 'Woman reports headless ostrich. Over.'

Endless hostage? Two Four Nine hesitated. What the hell is an endless hostage? A long siege I would have heard about notwithstanding the pitiful state hereabouts of police communications. He thumbed his speak button. 'Two Four Nine say again. Over.'

98

'Proceed to Vincent Street,' his control said through the bacon noises. 'Woman reports headless ostrich. Over.'

A headless hostage? Oh God, Two Four Nine groaned. My first messy homicide. He pressed his speak button and tried to keep the rising adrenalin from his voice. 'Message acknowledged. Proceeding Vincent Street. P.C. Two Four Nine. Out.'

He had been rattling shop door knobs. He returned to his transport. He checked his lights and pausing only to adjust his bicycle clips he began pedalling for Vincent Street. Dynamo blazing.

A few streets away, the brothers Wilkinson were parking their unlettered, battered blue Transit van in the darkest space available before taking their house-breaking implements for an evening stroll. Tony was driving, craning his neck now rearwards through the open sliding door, where the burly Morris was standing invisibly in deep shadow making hand signals for his brother's guidance.

'Back you come, Our Kid.'

The van bumped and grated. Tony swore.

'I was signalling for you to stop,' Morris growled.

'In the dark, you pillock.'

They locked up carefully, being alert to how many possibilities there were of losing personal property.

They went to church. It was Tony's idea. He had seen it one evening by late, golden sunlight and been profoundly moved.

'There should be more to our lives,' he was explaining to his brother as they made their way in the shadows, 'than breaking into clubs and other licensed premises. What we ought to do is take a look at what the church has to offer. For a start there's all that lead on the roof.'

'But I like breaking into clubs and licensed premises,' Morris protested. 'I should miss the fruit machines.'

'We're not missing anything. We'll get back to the fruit machines. We're expanding, that's all. The business which fails to expand is doomed.'

'I wish you hadn't said that word, Our Kid,' Morris confessed.

'Expand?' Tony sighed. His brother's mental processes

99

were like shackles round your ankles. 'What's wrong with saying expand? A flair for foul language like you've got – you're going to start worrying about words like expand!'

'Not that word. The other word you said.' Morris repeated it with doleful relish. 'Doomed. If we're going creeping round graveyards I wish you hadn't said, Doomed.'

They were at the churchyard. Beyond its low wall the nearer graves were visible by street light. Beyond these were darkness.

'I sincerely hope, Our Morris,' Tony eyed the impressive mass of his sibling, 'that you're not going to turn out to be a big girl.' He found himself being hoisted off his feet by a meaty grip on his throat. A squeeze so brotherly it was bringing tears to his eyes. And probably lots of little ruptured blood vessels, he realised in his pain and panic. 'Point taken,' he wheezed and signalled his earnest wish to be returned to the pavement.

'It's just that I don't go a lot,' Morris granted his brother's wish, 'for friggin' about with the supernatural.'

'Morris,' Tony squeezed the words through a windpipe still imprinted with the memory of his brother's fist. 'Lead is not friggin' supernatural.'

'I don't like where it is,' Morris eyed the graves and the outer darkness with suspicion.

'It's on a church roof, Morris. Churches are usually in churchyards. I'm sorry I can't find us a nice convenient little church in the middle of a club or licensed premises,' he wiped his eyes. 'They don't build 'em next to freakin' fruit machines.'

'It's creepy,' Morris grunted flatly.

'Never,' Tony vaulted the low wall. 'Would I send you anywhere I wouldn't go myself?' He wagged a finger of admonishment at Morris who was showing no signs of following over the wall. 'You have got to stop watching horror videos, Our Morris. Why can't you watch porn like anybody normal?'

'I like horror videos.'

'I don't mind you having an unnatural obsession within

100

reason,' Tony wagged the finger. 'But when it starts interfering with business . . .'

'I like it when the dead come to life.'

'Are you coming, Our Morris?'

'Over there? You must be friggin' joking.'

'Morris. Listen to me. Pay attention, Morris. Look at me. Don't stand there being shifty. This is real life, Morris.' Tony waved a hand expansively as if the graveyard and all it contained were his.

'Video's better,' Morris said flatly. 'I'm not friggin' about in graveyards after dark.'

'Be reasonable, Morris. We can't steal the lead in broad daylight.'

'I'm not going over that wall,' Morris vowed. 'I thought we were going to do what we always do. Break into licensed premises. I wouldn't have come if I'd known we weren't going to break into licensed premises.'

'You're being stupid, Our Morris.'

'I'm going back to the van. Unless you want to get the lead and bring it here. If you get the lead and bring it here I'll help you carry it home.'

'I can't do it on me own. It needs somebody up there with some muscle. Somebody strong. Fit.' He glared at his brother. 'Thick.'

'I'm going back to the van.'

Morris began walking. Behind him, Tony was pacing between the gravestones, waving his arms in frustration and muttering phrases not entirely brotherly.

Morris was feeling guilty but safer. Definitely safer with every step which took him further from the graveyard. He turned a corner. It felt even better. Then he heard footsteps coming.

With the caution habitual to those who frequent licensed premises after hours, Morris nipped back round the corner he had just turned and peeped from its cover, waiting to identify the feet approaching as constabulary or civilian.

Still in the churchyard, seated now petulantly on the edge of a gravestone where he was contemplating the fickleness of

101

kith, Tony heard his brother's scream. Suddenly keenly aware of his surroundings Tony rose, the hair of his nape upstanding. Morris screaming was unusual and thereby sinister. People around Morris screaming was commonplace given his habit of bending fingers the wrong way for amusement as others might play with Rubik's cube. But Morris screaming! It was suddenly cold. He could feel a dampness of dew through the soles of his sneakers. The graveyard smelled earthy and clammy.

A rapid soft tattoo of approaching sneakers and Morris came streaking out of the darkness. He cleared the low wall and clutched his brother in a fierce embrace.

'It's not true,' he said.

Tony shivered and wondered what could be out there that was so terrifying it could make his brother regard a graveyard as a refuge.

'I saw it, Our Kid,' Morris shuddered. 'It was walking. With no head. Just neck and feathers. This huge bird.'

A bird? At night? Tony's mind was racing through the options. What kind of birds are out at night? Owls? Are owls huge? The Owl of the Baskervilles?

'I wish,' Clegg said, soothing a palpitating heart, 'that people would stop screaming.' They calmed Pinkerton. 'That's one in Vincent Street and now here. Why are they doing it? You never used to hear people screaming in the street. I blame the E.E.C. It's another damn thing we've picked up from Europe.'

'Bloke in the distance behind us,' Compo reported. 'On a bike with a helmet on.'

'Bicycles,' Seymour corrected, 'do not have helmets on.'

Then it dawned. Three minds raced to the same conclusion. The unwisdom of flaunting your peacock in the path of the constabulary. They tugged at Pinkerton's throttle and accelerated round the corner.

* * *

102

Crouching low for security reasons behind the churchyard wall, the brothers Wilkinson were in conference with Tony (the brains) explaining to Morris (the muscle) the unlikelihood of occult intrusions into their Yorkshire scene.

'But I saw it, Our Kid.'

'Tricks of the light, Morris. On a fevered imagination. Now don't start grabbing me by the throat again. No offence is intended. I just want you to ask yourself why any creature from beyond the grave would want to come haunting hereabouts where everybody's half dead anyway.'

'Dracula came from Whitby,' Morris said.

'He wasn't born and bred there, was he? He could never have played for Yorkshire.'

'I bet Lancashire would have had him.'

'The only fiend consistently after people's blood round here, Our Morris, is Bickerdyke at the shop. There's your Yorkshire vampire. This is not Transylvania, Morris. Our werewolves would have to be whippets. And we wouldn't wear garlic to save our lives.'

'I saw it,' Morris insisted.

Tony sighed. A stubborn breed. They heard the sound of running feet. They peered over the wall. Tony stifled a scream.

'I told you. Clever beggar.' Morris had his moment of triumph before he was overwhelmed by his own terror. They crouched at the base of the wall, hugging each other, whimpering in fear.

One pair of unstreamlined, built-for-comfort, elderly boots, one pair of river-ruined suede shoes, two wellies and a Thing with claws travelling rapidly Wilkinsonwards, came bounding over the low wall in search of cover.

The brothers Wilkinson shrieked and rose to their feet. Compo, Clegg and Seymour panicked at the sudden apparition. All parties scattered for safety.

P.C. Two Four Nine rang his bell in warning as he took the corner at a speed appropriate to his first messy homicide. His calves aching from a recent climb he was bending low over his bars now as he applied full power. He came, tyres whistling,

103

down the gentle incline past the church and saw the Thing wandering among the gravestones, its headless neck turning obscenely as it tried to get its bearings.

A sound of falling policeman rent the night. Compo, Clegg and Seymour winced as they appeared from graveyard darkness to collect their peacock. They heard the constable rising and fled with Pinkerton.

P.C. Two Four Nine flung his mangled bicycle over the church wall and shone his torch around the gravestones. 'Come out,' he ordered. 'With your wings up and no funny business,' and he laughed to himself a trifle hysterically.

3

Nora's birthday dawned cloudy. The town under mist and a low cloud ceiling with a feel already about it of heat to come.

The sound of water in the pipes awakened Wally. She was downstairs, he realised, putting the kettle on for the day's first brew of tea. He stretched into off-limits areas of bed.

I would have brewed it for her. Brought her a cup to bed. It's her birthday. But there would have been endless suspicion if she realised I'd remembered. You forget their birthdays for a few years and they start taking you for granted. As if you're always going to forget it.

I wonder if there's a peacock in me shed. He went to the window. He couldn't see his shed for mist but everything sounded quiet. He padded back to bed.

Best if she thinks she has to wake me up. Lying there snoring on her birthday while she brings me a cuppa tea. Then she feels everything's right with the world. Everything in its place. In such small ways is it possible to be a comfort to her.

Their wedding photo was on the dressing table. He could see himself in khaki coming almost up to her shoulders. Maybe I was taller in them days. She looked thin under the 'forties hat. But determined. Always determined. You had to be to wear a hat like that. What a flair she's always had for

105

terrible hats. I hate it when we have to go to weddings. They seem to have a lot more to spend on weddings these days. Ours, on the catering side, was a bit thin. Funny thing is I felt safer, even in wartime, once she married me. He acknowledged his debt with a nod at the photograph. I'll say that for you, lass. You put an end to all uncertainty. I've always known exactly where I belong.

'Are you going to be there all day?'

He heard her coming. When she'd gone he raised his cup towards the cheap wartime frame.

In Wally's pigeon shed, Compo was asleep in the warmth of Pinkerton's feathers. Pinkerton rose warily to his feet as Wally entered. Compo reached in his sleep for the suddenly missing covers. Wally poked him awake with a boot toe. 'Have you been here all night?'

'Will tha please put me eiderdown back and bog off till it gets properly light,' Compo groaned.

'It is properly light. It's a bit misty that's all.' Wally was eyeing the peacock with respect. Pinkerton, without his silencer, was returning the inspection. Compo, reluctantly admitting that his beauty sleep was over, was sitting up now on his sack on the floor and searching his fag tin for the first tab of the day.

'I don't usually allow smoking in here,' Wally pointed out.

'Hey up!' Compo protested. 'It's not exactly the Maternity Clinic.'

'That's just what it is,' Wally was checking his nesting boxes. 'I've got birds sitting in here.' His eyes fell on a depleted sack of feed. 'How much of this stuff has he eaten?'

'I had to feed the poor beggar. He'd had a rough night.' Compo sighed at the memories. 'We all had a rough night.'

Nora heard the postwoman push the letters through the slot. She finished burnishing her sink and dried her hands before

106

going to pick up her mail. There was no hurry. It wasn't only husbands who forgot.

There was a colourful prepaid envelope inviting her to send her films for developing. There was an Electoral Registration form, and a bill for Water Rates. Taking a hard, ascetic almost pleasure in the completeness of the world's indifference she carried them back to the mantelpiece and busied herself with cleaning her brasses. She collected all the little ornaments on to her large brass tray and sat down with the Duraglit.

As she handled each one the memories came tumbling back to her. The frog was from Aunty Beth the year before she went in for the exploratory. Wilf had since remarried but it wasn't working. They seemed to go on holiday a lot. Always a bad sign. The kids had never taken to her. Edward was teaching now. Beth would have been proud.

Nora had bought the bumblebee on a day trip to Scarborough. Herself and Wally with the bike and sidecar. It must be thirty years ago. We used to go all over. It was raining. We had sandwiches in a shelter on the Marine Drive. Watching the sea through the railings. Wondering what was at the other side. It was hard to believe he'd been over there. Fighting. And not all that long since. And now here he was throwing his crusts for the seagulls. It seemed untidy but I didn't interfere. He'd fought for his country, the least I could do was let him feed its seagulls. They were picking up every bit anyway. And it wasn't as if anybody was watching.

The fish came from Edinburgh. It was me mother's mother's. Between us we've nearly polished its scales away. One little brass fish. It's going to see us all away.

Compo was leading Pinkerton towards Nora's front steps. Wally was accompanying but at a safe distance and carrying Compo's home-made greetings card.

Pinkerton halted at the steps. 'Come on!' Compo gave the lead a tug. 'Don't start going temperamental on me now.' Compo climbed another step. Pinkerton began to cluck but

107

remained where he was. 'Shurrup!' Compo signalled urgently. 'Keep thee voice down.' He winced in Wally's direction. 'If he goes off now he'll spoil the surprise.'

'Oh I don't know about that,' Wally prophesied. 'If he starts screaming it's not something she's going to take in her stride.'

'Give him a push,' Compo ordered.

'Where?' Wally enquired, genuinely baffled by the abundance of feathers at his end of things.

'Start lifting his feathers,' Compo instructed impatiently. 'Sorta work thee way in till tha finds summat solid.'

'Charming,' Wally sighed. 'And we all know what that's going to be.'

'Get on with it.'

Wally hung the greetings card by its shabby string on the railings and began lifting Pinkerton's magnificent train gingerly.

'It's not going to bite thee,' Compo sneered. 'Not from that end.'

'Just promise me one thing,' Wally said gloomily. 'That when me hand finds what it's looking for it's not going to be naked.'

Perhaps affronted by these liberties with his appendages, Pinkerton began climbing the steps. Wally was greatly relieved to leave unsolved another of life's little mysteries. Like the Scotchman's kilt it was something he had no desire to go prying into. He watched while Compo arranged Pinkerton to his best advantage outside Nora's front door.

'Bring the card,' Compo snapped his fingers.

They hung it round Pinkerton's neck. Torn from a shoebox and hand-lettered in felt-tip marker it said:

'HAPPY BIRTHDAY NORA.'

'Now what?' Wally asked.

'We ring the bell.' Compo grinned and gave Pinkerton an affectionate pat.

'Let me get clear first.' Wally went surprisingly nimbly down the steps.

'What's to go wrong?' Compo asked.

'I'm not sure she's going to be all that chuffed,' Wally

pointed, 'by what your peacock's just done to her front steps.'

'Oh that!' Compo waved a hand dismissively. 'Don't worry about that. I'll see to that when the excitement's over.'

'Half the excitement,' Wally warned, 'I promise you is going to be about that.'

'Rubbish,' Compo grinned confidently. He brushed himself free of a few of the recent night's traces. 'It's plain tha knows nowt about women.' He rang the bell.

Wally sought shelter. Compo tried to prod Pinkerton into displaying his tail. Pinkerton opened his beak in protest just as Nora opened the door. She was carrying the tray of brass ornaments. She dropped them as the peacock shrieked, and shrieked herself. Below stairs Wally winced. Compo tried to rescue the situation with a soothing grin.

'Happy birthday, lass.'

'You!' she shrieked. 'I should have known.'

Accepting the open door as an invitation, Pinkerton was making his way in. Nora backed away.

'Get it out! Take it out!'

But Compo was separated from the lead dangling from Pinkerton's neck by several yards of feathers. As he pushed forward to reach for the lead Pinkerton was pushed further in. Nora watched her possessions being engulfed by a tide of feathers.

Wally peeped through the railings. Saw Pinkerton's tail with a Compo clinging to it. Saw both disappear into the house. Heard Nora beginning to get good and mad. Heard Compo trying to explain. Heard a peacock shrieking as Pinkerton, to show his appreciation of this neat new environment, erected the full splendour of his display. Wally heard their excited voices babbling and the sounds of ornaments crashing. He scurried away. Heading for town and the relative calm of rush-hour traffic. The mist was clearing. It was going to be a good day. For keeping out of the way. He wondered who she'd kill first. The peacock or its jockey. Happy Birthday Nora!

* * *

109

'I've finished with her,' Compo announced dramatically through his chip butty. 'It's all over.'

They were in the Seven Shepherds, having a pub lunch and a rest from the labours of returning Pinkerton to his native heath, minus a few feathers but otherwise remarkably chipper. They had co-opted Wesley and his Land Rover for the purpose and the memory of collecting the bird from Compo's under the lash of Nora's tongue as she whizzed about removing peacock traces from her little palace, was still lying depressingly on their little party.

'I don't know why you had to drag me into it,' Wesley complained. 'I was perfectly happy lying under an old Hillman. These twits arrive and yank me away. Next minute I've got this dragon lady spitting smoke and flame at me.'

'Not just you,' Seymour winced at the memory. 'We were all getting a singeing.'

'But I'm just the driver, aren't I? I wasn't even involved.' Wesley sighed into his pint. 'I've never seen a woman in such a mood.'

'And on her birthday too,' Clegg said.

A little peeved that his dramatic announcement had aroused such indifference, Compo tried again. 'Well that's it. I've finished. Done. Ended. Gone. All through.'

'For which heaven be praised,' Seymour gave thanks. 'I was dreading having to watch you wolfing your way through another chip sandwich.'

'I don't mean finished eating,' Compo snarled. 'Pillock! I mean finished wi' Nora.' He folded his arms and struck a resolute pose while he waited for sounds of wonder and disbelief. Instead there was silence. 'Well?' he asked indignantly. 'Has nobody got anything to say?'

'Does that mean you've not finished eating?' Seymour asked cautiously. 'Because if you're going to start again I'm going to move.'

'Sit down, prawn. I've finished wi' that too.'

'Don't lie to me. Don't ever lie to me.' Seymour resumed his seat.

'I think I'll go home and do a bit of ironing,' Clegg said.

'Stuff me!' Compo exploded.

110

'I'd much rather iron,' Clegg watched Compo as he paced around his chair in frustration. 'And I don't like ironing.'

'What a mob,' Compo complained. 'Call theeselves mates? Me love life's in tatters.'

'Well at last he's dressed suitably for the part.' Seymour sipped his pint.

'Nobody cares.' Compo sat down again.

'Aw!' they all said.

'Twenty years unrequited love up the swanee and not a word of sympathy.'

'Aw!' they all said again.

'They don't believe me. They think I'm kidding.' Compo wagged a peacock-stained, chip butty-marked, lovelorn finger at the three grinning faces. 'I'll show thee. I'll show her.'

Bean-Peach was inspecting Wesley's progress on the chariot. He sighed unhappily in the eternal twilight of Wesley's shed. Even in that industrious gloom it was clear that the machine would never take prizes for elegance of line.

'It's not one of the great chariots,' Bean-Peach frowned.

'True,' Wesley agreed.

'I suppose it will look better on the day,' Bean-Peach suggested in tones replete with a lack of faith remarkable in one of his cloth.

'Oh aye,' Wesley confirmed in a manner equally uninspiring. 'She'll look better on the day.'

They looked at the thing for a moment in silence.

'Well, maybe not all that much better,' Wesley admitted. 'It's the best I can do given the tatty raw material. It's all academic anyway, Vicar. You haven't got a driver.'

'Not got a driver?' Bean-Peach expanded to his full height alarmingly beneath the shed's flimsy roof. Wesley blanched, fearful for his rickety structure under the pressure of this excess of vicar.

'Why don't we go in the house?' Wesley reached out to steer Bean-Peach through the door. The vicar backed hastily from the advancing, oily hand, thinking – it's all very well this

111

shepherding one's flock but they do tend to stain one unless one keeps a distance. 'I believe the wife's buttering some plumcake for us.' Wesley felt the vicar flinch beneath his touch. Why, he wondered? Is the man so nervous of plumcake?

Edie greeted Bean-Peach with her full ceremonial as befitted his rating on her social scale. She seated him comfortably in the best armchair. Wesley she made stand on a newspaper. She left in pursuance of plumcake.

'No driver!' Bean-Peach glared at Wesley. 'I thought we'd enrolled the unsightly, small chap. I distinctly remember my telling him he was going to do it.'

'Wasn't what you'd call expert, was he?'

'He was terrible,' Bean-Peach conceded. 'But I assumed he'd have the decency to practise.'

Wesley shook his head. His cap slid. He returned it. 'He doesn't go in much for dogged determination. He's more your spontaneous, instinctive, totally unreliable type.'

'Well, it's a damn bad show.' Wesley shifted uneasily on his newspaper, feeling guilty by association. Bean-Peach looked at the spotless frills of Edie's settee and had an idea. 'We could dress the machine up as a ladies' chariot. Ladies used to drive chariots. There was Queen Boadicea.'

'Oh aye,' Wesley agreed. 'There was Queen Boadicea.'

'That's what we'll do then.' Bean-Peach felt better already. 'Rosemary will have to drive it.'

The sign at the former chapel said 'The Norris and Esme Wright School of Dance'. It was in Chapel Street. Not, Clegg noted, since renamed Norris and Esme Wright School of Dance Street. Chapel Street ran steeply and narrowly in a curve down to High Street busy with afternoon shoppers, but Chapel Street was quiet. The chapel was next to Andy's Budget Remould Tyres. Now defunct. A faded day-glo 'Prices Slashed' poster still visible in the vandalised interior.

They took a breather from their climb at the stone wall on

112

the opposite side of the street. They sat and contemplated the chapel. Clegg, Compo, Seymour; Wesley – to the best of their knowledge – back under his Hillman. Behind and below them a steep weedy bank descended to the pocket back-gardens, sheds and miscellany of garages of Milton Street. Pigeons were wheeling in formation. They could hear kids shrieking in Milton Street schoolyard.

'I'm going in,' Compo sounded like John Wayne about to go over the top.

'I like your dancing shoes,' Clegg glanced at Compo's wellies.

'Not to dance, you muffin. For the other thing.'

Clegg and Seymour exchanged a startled glance.

'They fix people up,' Compo explained.

'You could use a bit,' Seymour admitted.

'With partners,' Compo elaborated. 'Of the opposite sex.' He tugged them from the wall and led them across the road to where they could read the smaller print of the School of Dance sign. The smaller print said 'Incorporating the Norris and Esme Wright Rainbow Circle for Friendship and Marriage'.

'Shouldn't it be friendship *or* marriage?' Clegg enquired.

'Don't be cynical,' Seymour reproved. 'There is a place, I feel, for this kind of service which can pair suitable people together. It takes much of the element of risk away. I have myself, on occasion, considered submitting my requirements.'

'I'm going in,' Compo said. 'It's no good moping about out here. When there's a great hole in thee life the best thing to do is get it filled in.'

'Fill these in,' the woman instructed. She was late middle-aged and stout with glasses, through which her magnified eyes were staring in some alarm at Compo's appearance. 'Name, address and occupation in block capitals. The rest write neatly, please. Remember people have to try and read it.'

113

She proffered three printed forms. 'Not me,' Clegg backed away. 'I'm just browsing.'

She showed them to a former chapel table to which a ballpoint pen was attached by a chain. She left them on former chapel chairs and went back through the door their entrance had produced her from.

'She's a big lass,' Compo said. 'I wonder if she's spoken for.'

They were in a flimsily partitioned segment of a larger room. Through the walls they could hear Victor Sylvester being stopped and started at the whims of Norris and Esme. The walls were hung with photographs of Norris and Esme recording the triumphs of a glittering career. The floorboards were bare. Sunlight was straining through the opaque grimy chapel window and in its angled and diluted beam motes were dancing without reference to Norris and Esme.

'Bags the pen,' Compo snatched it and rattled the chain.

'I have my own,' Seymour produced a more headmasterly instrument. They settled down to their respective forms.

Clegg was filled with a vague unease. He found the ambience depressing. A place for army medicals. A situation only to be conscripted to. And here he was with two lunatic volunteers.

He studied the photographs.

Norris and Esme were quite famous locally, she for the startling orange of her hair and her affectedness, he for being the poor prawn she was married to though his own affectations were prodigious. And together they were locally renowned for the display of marital bliss they mounted sickeningly on all public occasions. This campaign to perpetuate the legend of the flawlessness of their partnership in both ballroom and bedroom, with its public embraces and 'darlings', had led to their nickname as the Conjugal Wrights.

'How does tha spell boobs?' Compo was sucking the pen on the end of its chain and looking unhappy at all the paperwork he had suddenly stumbled into.

Seymour hastily snatched Compo's form.

'Hey up! I haven't finished.'

Seymour was reading the blotchy scrawl with increasing

114

alarm. 'God in heaven, man! You can't write things like that.'

'Listen, Big Shirley,' Compo wagged the pen at Seymour. 'Thee pick what tha thinks is important. Leave me to pick what— '

Seymour crumpled Compo's romantic specifications into a ball and buried them in a pocket. 'Get him a new form,' he ordered Clegg. 'Help him fill it in.'

Clegg knocked reluctantly on the stout woman's door. Norris Wright opened it, handsome in velvet jacket and Grecian 2000.

'Could I have another application form,' Clegg mumbled, 'for the Rainbow Circle?'

Norris flashed his capped teeth in a glittering smile. He placed a sympathetic, unworksoiled hand on Clegg's shoulder. 'Another one? That's the spirit. If at first,' he said, giving the impression of a phrase newly minted, 'we don't succeed.' He bent a cared-for face towards Clegg's startled, homely features. Clegg fell under the spell of a powerful aftershave. 'Love,' Norris confided, 'wasn't built in a day.' He removed the sympathetic hand, and wiped it vigorously on a snowy handkerchief. 'But give us time and we'll find you a Mrs Right. Not my Mrs Wright,' he laughed appreciatively at a gag which had served him many times.

'It's not for me,' Clegg blushed. 'I'm just collecting it for a friend.'

'You wouldn't believe how many say that,' Norris looked wise, as he handed Clegg another application form. 'Those who suffer from the national disease.'

'If you're worried about the spot,' Clegg said, touching the place. 'It's only a pimple. You get 'em occasionally.'

'The national disease,' Norris continued, 'of suppressing natural feelings. They come creeping in here, Little Grey People.' He fixed Clegg with a dancing master's stare. 'Stop being a grey person. Turn on to Life. Turn out. Get unbuttoned. That is the rhythm for your life. That is what you have learned already from Norris and Esme Wright. Name,

115

address and occupation in block capitals. The rest write neatly, please. Remember people have to try and read it. Give us a knock when you've finished and we'll see you for the interview.'

He withdrew, closing the door in Clegg's face before Clegg could establish his non-playing status. Grumbling, Clegg took the form back to the table where Compo was waiting. 'I like being a grey person,' Clegg said.

'Tha writes me name, address and occupation in block capitals,' Compo instructed.

'Shurrup!' Clegg snapped.

'Temper.'

'Some of us have spent years becoming little grey people. Then he comes along with his glittering teeth. What do you want me to put down under occupation?'

'Company Director,' Compo said promptly.

Seymour snorted. 'It's no good lying so obviously.'

'Retired,' Compo amended. 'All right,' he conceded. 'If we're going to be honest. Put Civil Servant.'

'What's honest about that?'

'The D.H.S.S.' Compo said haughtily, 'have been paying my salary for years.'

You couldn't argue with that.

Seymour went first for his interview. He was shown, by the stout woman, to a door at which he knocked.

'Come in,' an orange-haired voice invited with immense articulation. Seymour entered. 'Do sit down,' the orange creature said, an orange mouth performing prodigies of elocution which Seymour felt must surely crack the icing of her make-up. She was holding hands with Norris. They were standing posed matrimonially in the light from the large chapel window. The radiance of their combined teeth was echoed in their photographs around the walls. Large professional blow-ups this time of the smaller prints outside. She waved long, orange fingernails ballroom-balletically to indi-

116

cate the chair before the desk where Seymour should sit. He lowered his tall frame into it.

'Welcome,' she said, 'to the Rainbow Circle. We are Norris and Esme Wright.' It was something he'd never really doubted. They hadn't moved except to face each other with the smiles as she made the introduction. It gave the impression that being Norris and Esme Wright was a source of endless satisfaction to them. Seymour half expected the music to strike up and they would begin to dance.

Instead the smiles went and they moved brisk and businesslike into identical chairs across the desk from Seymour. They both produced reading glasses which had the effect of seeming to reduce them considerably in size as they scanned through Seymour's application form.

'Educated,' Esme muttered.

'Good professional background,' Norris mumbled. 'Looks like he'll be Executive. Category Two.'

'What's wrong with Category One?' Seymour enquired.

Esme flashed a brief smile, gone instantly as if the orange lips were zipped. 'We've never had a Category One, Mister – Otterthwaite.'

'Utterthwaite,' Seymour corrected.

She flashed a hard, unballroom look at Norris and made a small amendment to Seymour's form.

'I told the other one block capitals,' a chastened Norris said.

'If you've never had a Category One—' Seymour persisted.

'In all our years,' Norris said and the cue was picked up deftly on the instant and they turned in perfect unison to take a smile. 'Not one Category One.'

'Then perhaps you should start upgrading a few of us better Category Twos.'

'Category One,' Esme removed her glasses and smiled without warmth at Seymour, 'is reserved for persons of means.'

'I'm looking for just such a person. You've got it right there in front of you. Under "any special requirements".'

117

'For persons of means,' Esme added, 'who do not need to look for persons of means.'

'It would be very short-sighted to overlook my potential,' Seymour explained. 'I have enormous prospects. A little seed money. Some development capital and I'm away. I have a self-propelled wheelbarrow ready for marketing.'

The Conjugal Wrights exchanged a tired look absent from all the photographs.

'I am prepared to lay my genius at the feet of any suitably qualified lady of acceptable appearance.'

'Next,' the stout woman announced. Compo rose and had Clegg check him out for pigeon and peacock leavings.

'Maybe I should have gone home first and changed,' Compo conceded.

'Preferably into somebody younger and taller,' Clegg said.

'Come in wi' me, Norm,' Compo clutched Clegg.

'Gerroff!' Clegg tried to break free.

'Just to see fair play,' Compo wheedled. 'Tha dunt have to join.'

'Seymour went in,' Clegg pointed out. 'We haven't seen him since.'

'They can't have married him off already. Not a long prong like that.'

'He went out the front,' the stout woman said. 'To have a sulk I think. Are you coming or aren't you?'

'It looks like we're coming,' Clegg sighed as he was towed by Compo in the wake of the stout woman.

'This should make her day,' she was smiling as she rapped on the door.

'Enter,' the orange-coloured voice said.

'Listen,' Compo said to the stout woman on his way in. 'If there's nowt better inside, how about thee and me having a drink some night?'

'Who's your silver-tongued friend?' she asked of Clegg as he was dragged in. She closed the door and applied her ear.

118

* * *

The smiles of the Conjugal Wrights congealed on their faces in the chapel window light.

'How do,' Compo nodded.

Clegg removed his cap and shuffled a smile through his embarrassment.

The pose by the window collapsed. Esme came hastily forward to check the new form on her desk.

'I never saw that one,' the shaken Norris whispered. 'I don't know who let him in. I only saw him.' He indicated Clegg.

'Which one of you,' Esme enquired, articulation shot, 'is Simmonite?'

'That's me, missis,' Compo gave her a wink. 'He's just come for company like.'

'I could wait outside.' Clegg began edging towards the door and was hauled back by Compo.

Enormously gratified that her new client had turned out to be the weird one, Esme skewered Norris with a glance.

'We're going to have to open a new category.' Norris shrugged away the responsibility.

'Perhaps there's some mistake,' Esme mumbled. 'Does he realise what it is we do here?'

'Judging by what's down here,' Norris was gaping at the form. 'He had a damn good idea.'

'You do realise, Mister – er – Simmonite,' Esme smiled pluckily and recovered some articulation. 'That we are here to help people form lasting relationships.'

'Just what I'm after,' Compo sat in the chair and crossed his wellies. 'I'm between relationships. I've just finished wi' one that's been going on for years.' He sighed. 'She was tall,' he said. 'A lovely sweeper. She kept her yard cleaner than some of my plates.'

The Wrights were not listening but had reversed to a far corner by a filing cabinet where they were engaged in the delicate footwork of a whispered negotiation. Esme was

119

leading. That its subject was Compo became plain as each kept twirling the skirts of a glance across him, Norris with alarm, Esme with appraisal.

Clegg bent to whisper in Compo's ear. 'Stop showing off. How long have you had more than one plate?'

'I'll get two,' Compo promised. 'Soon as they fix me up wi' a lasting relationship.'

'Mister Simmonite,' Esme came forward again, this time with more wattage in her smile. 'Would you agree to be photographed?'

Compo and Clegg exchanged a look of surprise. Compo glanced down at his appearance. 'They don't allus flatter me,' he confessed. 'I think I'd probably do better if tha lets me meet a few birds first in the flesh.' He was picking at a pigeon stain. 'If tha starts showin' 'em photos they could turn negative which would be a pity becos they've never felt the full force of me personality.'

'What I have in mind,' Esme explained, 'are photographs not just for your file, but for our own publicity purposes. You'd be excellent as the star in a Before and After sequence.'

'As the star,' Compo repeated, not displeased.

'Wouldn't he, darling?' Esme smiled instinctively at the less certain Norris. 'Can't you see him?'

'I've never seen a more startling Before,' Norris shuddered.

'Absolutely,' Esme trilled with enthusiasm for her idea. 'The contrast, if we have him taken now. Just as he is.'

'I could nip home and get done up a bit,' Compo offered.

'No!' Esme rattled the window with alarm.

'I mebbe ought to have done before I came,' Compo admitted.

'Absolutely not,' Esme said, yanking Norris back to the filing cabinet for a further quadrille of convincing.

'But tha knows how it is,' Compo sighed. 'A bloke drops into these places on the spur o' the moment. With his bruised feelings.'

Clegg mimed the gesture of wiping a tear. Compo's spirits returned with a leap. He dug Clegg with an elbow. 'A star,' he chuckled. 'How about that then?'

120

Clegg didn't reply since he was fully engrossed in trying to quell the pain occasioned by Compo's wild elbow. In not making allowances for the fact that he was seated, while Clegg remained standing, Compo's sharp elbow had flicked like a billiard cue, not into its usual target, but this time into another pocket area entirely. Clegg was now finding real tears and experiencing a bundle of reasons against remaining upright.

'That's settled then,' Esme announced, returning with the smile, and the look on Norris's face confirmed that it was. 'The contrast,' Esme enthused, 'between the rejected, unwanted, neglected Mister Simmonite as he is now—' She half-circled Compo in his chair. He was really unbelievable. The clothes. My God. He looks as if he's been sleeping with the pigeons or something. 'And the restored and happy figure he will become because he had the wisdom to place himself in the arms of the Rainbow Circle.'

I'm being very moving she realised as she returned to her chair. There are tears in the eyes of his friend. 'We shall give you polish, Mister Simmonite,' she promised as she scribbled a note on letter-headed paper.

Polish? Compo sighed. Have I got to clean up? Does that mean when they find me a bird she'll be coming to my place? Hey up! I should have been on this lark yonks ago. On the other hand, I see no reason yet to start acting panicky and cleaning up. Why can't we go to her place. Let her clean up.

'Has tha got somebody in mind for me?'

'What type did you have in mind, Mister Simmonite?' Esme enquired to cover the fact that she couldn't imagine where any such creature might be found.

Compo gave his answer some serious thought. He screwed up his unshaven face in deep contemplation. It was a hard one. And Clegg was no help. What type of woman would a bloke need? It was no good fantasising. It was time for realism. They were down to the nitty gritty.

'Has tha got anything,' he finally broke his silence, 'wi' wrinkled stockings?'

But the Conjugal Wrights were not listening. They were

121

hunting somewhat desperately through their filing cabinet.

'There's no one,' Norris surrendered.

'There must be someone,' Esme was made of sterner stuff. 'For starters anyway. Think, darling. Use your brain. What an absolutely golden opportunity to get our own back on some unpleasant female timewaster.' They paused as if zapped by a ray gun, sci-fi still. With that instinctive mutual timing which had made them the darlings of judges now retired in Huddersfield their mouths moved as one as they enunciated the magic name.

'Mrs Jack Halliwell.'

'Dare we?' Norris was in love already with the idea.

Esme produced the Halliwell folder. Thicker than most. 'It's a natural,' she breathed, holding the folder to a suddenly palpitating very flat chest.

'The very partner for you,' Esme advanced on Compo. He reached for the folder. She tugged away. 'First things first.'

She sealed the note she had written into an envelope. 'You will take this, now, to West Yorkshire Society Photographers in Crabb Street. He does all our artwork. No cheating now,' she admonished. 'Just as I see you here. No titivating. I'm relying on your friend to support me.' He doesn't look very reliable she noted. Swaying like that. They have all, of course, been drinking.

'Tonight is the time for sprucing up. It's best frocks and manners. We prefer our men in dinner jackets. However,' she frowned at the hopelessness of the idea, 'your best efforts will be acceptable. For our Rainbow Circle Weekly Social Evening. To which you are all invited. Lucky men.' She tapped the folder. 'To meet our ladies. Seven thirty till nine.'

They were dismissed.

Seymour did indeed seem a little miffed as they made their way to Crabb Street. 'It wasn't the welcome I anticipated,' he admitted. 'They seemed curiously lacking in any real perceptiveness. Why are you walking like that, Clegg?'

122

'It doesn't matter,' Clegg said. 'It's nearly better now.' He glared at the oblivious Compo who was clutching Esme's letter in his fist.

'They're getting me a Mrs Jack Halliwell,' Compo informed Seymour. 'Soon as one comes in.'

'I shouldn't get too excited,' Seymour warned. 'Their judgement's bound to be shaky if they can't recognise a Category One when they see one.'

'What's tha going to wear then tonight, Cleggy?'

'Pyjamas,' Clegg said firmly. 'I'm going early to bed.'

'It's finished at nine,' Compo protested. 'Then tha can go to bed.'

'You must join us, Clegg,' Seymour ordered. 'It would be an extremely bad first move, tactically, for me to appear alone with him.' He scowled at Compo.

'Hey up, Gladys. Tonight I shall be all tarted up. Tha'll not recognise me.'

'I certainly intend not to.'

'Tha'll have to come to keep the peace, Norm. Tha sees what a pain in the pussy he's going to be.'

'No,' Clegg vowed. 'I should be terrified.'

'Tha's only window shopping. Tha's not actually buying.'

'All you'll have to do at the most,' Seymour encouraged, 'is exchange a polite word when spoken to.'

'That,' Clegg said, 'is how I got married last time.'

West Yorkshire Society Photographers in Crabb Street was remarkable mainly for the fact that several of the portraits in its window were upside down. Otherwise it was just a shop front and rear studio in a converted terrace house with living accommodation over.

As they stood before its window, their heads twisted awkwardly, the tall, balding proprietor with a face of great sadness and solemnity appeared with the very centrepiece of his display – a bridal portrait on a small easel. He proceeded to arrange it fussily – ignoring their stares with the artist's

123

sovereign contempt for his audience. After several moments, satisfied, he withdrew. They looked at the bride. She was upside down.

'The man has a certain flair,' Seymour acknowledged, 'for display. A trifle obvious yet it does, unquestionably, seize the attention.'

'If I were the groom,' Compo snorted, 'I wouldn't want my bride upending in Crabb Street.'

'I can see it now,' Clegg said. 'Mrs Jack Halliwell upside down in Crabb Street.'

'Bog off!' the latest member of the Rainbow Circle said.

A bell above the door tinkled as they went in. The tall, sad man appeared from behind curtains in the rear. He stood at his small counter. There was a strong smell of peppermints. He seemed to be having some difficulty in focusing on Compo. He closed one eye. Still dissatisfied he opened it and closed the other. It seemed no better.

'What's up wi' thee then?' Compo was becoming offended.

'It's my eyes,' the man said, a sad voice rising in panic. 'Excuse me.' He disappeared behind the curtain.

They exchanged glances.

'Maybe he's O.D.'d,' Clegg suggested. 'On peppermints.'

They jumped as the curtain twitched and the man returned, a portrait lens to his eye that he was focusing on Compo as he came.

'Say cheese,' Clegg advised.

But the man was lowering the lens in profound relief. 'Thank God,' he breathed, leaning weakly across his counter. 'He looked all blurred and muzzy. I thought it was my eyes. I see now,' he was recovering his composure. He frowned at Compo's appearance. 'He really is all blurred and muzzy.'

'Listen, twithead,' Compo began and found his mouth temporarily sealed by Clegg's hand.

'He's had a rough night,' Clegg explained hastily before Compo could get his invective into gear.

'Don't apologise,' the man said. 'I'm just glad it's him that's blurred and muzzy and not my eyes.'

'We have a note,' Seymour snatched the envelope and read

124

it. 'For the hand of a Mister Cyril Nugent of this address.'

'Me,' he held his hand out for the note. 'Sole owner and proprietor.'

'I'm going to be a star,' Compo said. 'Of a Before and After. And if it's all the same to thee, I'd like both to be right way up.'

'What's he on about?' Nugent muttered as he read the note.

'He's unfamiliar,' Seymour said patronisingly, 'with the concept of artistic licence in display.'

Nugent turned to Clegg. 'What are they both on about?'

'To the casual window gazer,' Clegg explained, 'it would appear that several of your items are upside down.'

'Never!' Nugent was appalled. He went outside. Before the bell had stopped tinkling it tinkled again as he returned, shamefaced and apologetic. 'You feel such a fool,' he began repairing his display, groaning each time he found another one. 'Oh God, I wonder how long this has been going on. You know what it is, don't you?' he told them when he'd finished and could turn his attention back to them.

'Tha's been knocking back a few,' Compo accused, sniffing his way through peppermint to a familiar base flavour.

'I've just done a wedding,' Nugent admitted. 'They're always pouring it down you. You know what they're like round here at weddings. There's so much booze thrown about it can fell the innocent along with the guilty. It's not that though. I'm not a big drinker.' He stifled a burp sadly. 'Ever since me hair fell out,' he confessed, 'I've tried to live abstemiously. No, what it is,' he sighed, 'is a cry for help.'

He took them through into the studio and began lighting Compo to his worst advantage.

'Don't ask me to smile,' Compo said. 'Not today. Me and the woman next door's just broken it off after all these years.'

'You can see her point though, can't you?' Nugent said as he peered professionally at his subject. 'They've overdone it,' he shook his head. 'I don't know who made you up like this but they've gone way over the top.'

125

'Naff off!' Compo was touched to the quick. 'It's all genuine is this.'

'He's having me on,' Nugent looked to Clegg and Seymour for confirmation. They shook their heads.

Outside the Polaroid Kid had his nose pressed to the camera window. A dog called Vince, an old black labrador with a grey muzzle, was examining a fish and chip paper. Somebody's grandmother was sitting on a chair on the pavement in the afternoon sunlight. The road smelled of tar.

It was still warm in the early evening, despite which, Wally stepped out from his front door in his huge, all weather, motor-cycling coat, helmet tucked under his arm. He paused on the steps to sniff what the sky was offering. He looked like a medieval knight. Campaign worn. Weary. A very small medieval knight superbly adapted to that bleak period.

He came down the steps, his over-trousers whistling water-repellently as Compo came up from his front door.

'How do, Compo,' Wally said wistfully, then stopped to take a better look. This was a Compo transformed.

'How do thee sen, Wally,' Compo nodded. His face shiny, clean-shaven and nicked in several places. His hair snug as a bathing cap under the weight of solid brilliantine. He was wearing a dark-blue suit with a rather forceful chalk stripe, a new turquoise shirt and a black tie. He smelled powerfully of a high-octane mix of brilliantine and aftershave. The suit was over-large, the freshly whitened sneakers on his feet perhaps a mistake but there was no argument, Wally conceded. He's really tried.

'What's tha think then, Wal?' Compo enquired a mite anxiously, doing a pirouette to give Wally the full flavour.

'It's beautiful,' Wally said, genuinely impressed.

'I usually go for flash,' Compo admitted. 'But this time I went for formal and sober.'

126

'Good thinking,' Wally approved.

'I've not overdone it, have I?' Compo asked, fingering the black tie.

'I wouldn't change a thing. 'Cept maybe the shoes.'

'I know,' Compo admitted. 'I've got no black shoes.'

'I'd lend you mine,' Wally offered. 'But I'm wearing 'em. I'm taking Nora for a birthday meal.' He sighed. 'I'd much sooner lend 'em to you and have to stop in.'

'Not to worry, old Wal,' Compo patted Wally on the motoring coat. It was like hitting a tree. 'I'll be all right wi' these. At least they're clean.'

'Oh aye, they're clean,' Wally admitted.

'And they'll be handy for dancing in.' Compo noted Wally's look of surprise. 'I've joined the Rainbow Circle, Wal. It's all over between me and your missis.'

Compo was startled to find himself being clutched by Wally, fiercely.

'You swine!'

'Wally!'

'Call yourself a neighbour.'

'Mind the suit, Wally.'

'You think you can trust people.' He released his grip on Compo and began pacing clumsily in his whistling over-trousers. Compo straightened his suit and backed away as the medieval knight bore down on him again, face wild with emotion.

'You can't chicken out on her now,' Wally pleaded. 'Not after all these years. You can't just leave her with nothing to moan about but me.' He was reaching for the suit again. Compo turned nimbly on flashing sneakers.

'It's her birthday.' Wally gave up the pursuit and leaned weakly against the steps. 'What kind of unscrupulous twot would abandon my missis on her birthday?'

'She threw me out,' Compo protested. 'She got really nasty.'

'A little tiff,' Wally said. 'A bit of cross purposes over a peacock. If nothing else I wish you'd spare a thought for my position. There's been hell on all day. Maybe,' Wally said, clutching at straws, 'she's already sorry you've gone.'

127

'Does tha reckon?' Compo was much pleased with the idea.

'She'll be out in a minute,' Wally said. 'All done up for a birthday dinner. Make it up, why don't you? Somebody's got to make the first move. Why not me? I'll steer her past your steps. Then you can leap out and throw yourself on her mercy.'

'It's times like this,' Compo said deeply affected, 'tha learns who thee mates are.' They shook hands, powerfully moved. Compo went back to the cover of his steps. Wally returned to the foot of his own as they heard her come out and stop to lock the door.

'Did I turn the immersion off?' she asked.

'You always do,' Wally said.

'I'd better check,' she reopened the door. 'Fat lot you care. It could bubble away all night if it was left to you.' She went back in. Wally signalled Compo to stay where he was.

She came out again and relocked the door. 'It was off,' she admitted.

'I knew it would be.'

'You have to check.' She adjusted her hat. It was duck-egg blue. 'You can't evade your responsibilities,' she said, coming carefully in her best shoes down the steps.

He proffered his arm when she got to the bottom. She gave him a look of sharp enquiry. 'Put it away,' she ordered. 'I'm sure we're not starting mauling each other about at our age. I hate to see it in the street. People mauling each other about.'

He followed in her wake thinking, I wish she wouldn't wear duck-egg blue. His trousers whispered repellently.

'I wish you'd keep your trousers quiet,' she scolded. 'We don't want him to hear us.' She jumped as Compo leapt out nimbly on silent white feet over which the too-long trousers were concertina'd.

'Give us a kiss for thee birthday.'

Her nose went up to the duck-egg blue. 'Are you going to stand there,' she demanded of her husband, 'and let him insult me?'

128

'They serve meals till nine,' Wally pointed out reasonably. 'We've got plenty of time.'

'Oh,' she groaned in frustration. 'You've never been a prop I could rely on in physical emergencies.'

'No lass,' Wally agreed, trying to sweeten the emotional atmosphere. 'But you always have been for me.' He received a not unexpected blow from her best handbag.

'Like that then, is it?' Compo said jealously. 'He gets the clout wi' the handbag these days. Do I take it tha's stopped offering violence to me?'

'I haven't time,' she said, nose back in the duck-egg blue, 'to bandy words out here. When we're on our way to a proper sit-down knife and fork meal. With starters and sweet course – and – ' she added the clincher, 'even possibly wine.'

Wally's eyebrows shot up in surprise. 'Can I stick to beer?'

'Shut up,' she ordered. 'It's my birthday. You'll drink what you're told.' She made a regal detour around Compo.

'All right,' he said. 'If that's how tha wants it. Don't blame me,' he shouted as she went like Britannia round the corner, 'if tha finds me drowning me sorrows wi' a Mrs Jack Halliwell.'

'Don't do anything rash,' Wally pleaded. 'She'll come round.' And she did. She came back round the corner to speed up her husband.

'Are we going or aren't we? Move!'

He moved. As fast as his motoring coat and whispering trousers would let him.

'Oh my God!' Seymour rose to his feet in alarm at Compo's appearance as Clegg led him into his sitting room. Seymour took a turn round the chalk stripes, his eyes wide with premonitions of social disaster. Seymour was in his dinner jacket. Clegg, much against his will, in his best clerical grey (distinguishable from his usual clerical grey chiefly by the fact that he looked uncomfortable in it).

'I got it,' Compo announced proudly, 'from Dudley's Nearly New Shop wi' that money we made last night flogging

129

chips at the Armpit Millionaire's. Money which otherwise I should probably only have wasted.'

'Oh my God!' Seymour repeated, sinking back into his chair.

'You seem to have done something radical with your hair,' Clegg said, sniffing cautiously. 'Like removing it and having your head sprayed. You're obviously working on the principle that nothing is too much trouble for Mrs Jack Halliwell.'

'I am,' Compo admitted. 'I just hope she has the sense to appreciate it.'

'Why has he got those gravy boat things on his feet?' Seymour's voice was heavy with pain.

'I hope tha dunt think I were going to turn up to me first Rainbow Circle in wellies.' Compo was deeply offended. 'I admit they're me old sneakers but they're freshly painted.'

'And it's coming off,' Clegg pointed to the marks on his rug with alarm.

'Oh stuff me! It's on me trousers.' Compo hauled up the lengthy garments to reveal for the first time a pair of electric pink socks. Seymour covered his eyes. Compo sat on the arm of Clegg's settee and began trying to brush away the powdery white stains.

'Take 'em off,' Clegg suggested, fearful for his furniture. Soon the pink socks were revealed in all their glory.

'Stand up!' Seymour ordered. Compo obliged. The trousers fell magically to extinguish the flamboyant hosiery. 'Thank goodness for small mercies,' Seymour snarled through clenched teeth. 'Stay like that.' He turned to Clegg. 'You're going to have to lend him some black shoes.'

'We've tried it before. Mine don't fit him.'

They went next door to Howard's. Howard was a neighbour of suitable dimensions.

'He's not in,' Pearl said, glaring at the three figures on her doorstep with two pairs of shoes between them. 'He's out in that damned chip van you talked him into.'

'Money grabber,' Compo grinned.

'It better be all he's grabbing,' Pearl said. 'And if you see that Marina you can tell her. She best not let me catch her smelling of chips.'

'I'm sure your husband, madam,' Seymour smiled encouragingly, 'has only the highest commercial motives.'

'Pull the other one,' she said. 'And he has no black shoes. He's bought only suede lately. Another indicator for those who can read. When some old fool's fancy turns lightly to thoughts of suede. Wait on!' she ordered. 'Stand there.' She left them at the open doorway. Compo picked a piece of gravel from his stocking foot.

'Don't point that damn thing at me,' Seymour objected. 'Put it away.'

'Why that colour?' Clegg asked.

'It were Dudley's idea,' Compo acknowledged. 'They were very reasonable.'

Pearl returned with a pair of fine, sturdy black Oxfords, still uncreased in their shoe trees. 'Here,' she said. 'You can take these. They were me father's. We were going to bury him in them. But it seemed a shame. I said they'd come in useful to somebody.'

She cut short their thanks by closing the door.

'Hey up,' Compo approved. 'How about these then?'

'Don't sit in the street,' Seymour hauled Compo upright. 'You can put them on next door.'

They returned to Clegg's, Compo much impressed with his elevation to serious footwear. Seymour vastly relieved at the prospect of sneakers superseded. Clegg grateful for any promise of a quieter life.

'Hey up! They're a bit of first class are these.' Compo admired the sturdy, fine leather still taut in the shoe trees. 'They've had no wear at all haven't these.' He buffed the toes lovingly with a chalk-striped sleeve.

'Will you please put them on and hide those technicolour

131

feet.' Seymour thrust Compo into Clegg's fireside chair.

'They're newish shoes, man.' Seymour seized the left one from the floor and began to demonstrate the stiffness of its leather. 'You'd be in terrible trouble if they were tight.'

Clegg returned with a pair of clean, serviceable, thick, grey woollen socks. Seymour was much relieved to see these decent veils being drawn over the electric-pink nightmares.

The shoes went on again. Clegg laced them tightly. Seymour muttered a small prayer to whatever powers may govern the luck of inventors intent on marrying some development money.

Compo stood and took a few trial paces. The shoes went with him.

'That's near enough,' Seymour gave judgement and hustled them quickly out of the house.

What had not been noticeable on Clegg's carpet became quickly apparent on the pavement. The noise. Compo's progress was marked by an unseemly slapping sound. Each time a foot came down it was with a smack like a table-tennis bat.

They stopped. The noise stopped. Seymour glared angrily. Compo shrugged. They walked on. The slaps began again.

Clegg separated Seymour from Compo's throat. 'He's not trying,' Seymour snarled.

'I'm walking quiet,' Compo said. 'What the 'ell the shoes are doing, God knows.'

'Point your toes,' Seymour ordered, and gave a demonstration which was much appreciated by four young men whose passing vehicle made him jump with alarm as they hooted and cheered.

'Tha can make an exhibition of thee sen if tha likes,' Compo said haughtily. 'But not me.'

They walked on towards the bus stop, Seymour wincing at every slap.

'Don't look at me,' Compo said. ' 'They're completely

132

beyond me control. I wonder,' he turned to Clegg, 'what size Pearl's father was.'

'I don't know,' Clegg said. 'But I bet he died from terminal noisy feet.'

'They don't look bad,' Seymour said as they crossed the road. 'If only you could keep them down a bit.' They saw the bus coming. They had to run for it. The manoeuvre drew first startled then amused looks from the queue at the bus stop.

'Come on then, Twinkletoes,' somebody shouted.

'Bog off!' Compo panted.

They boarded the bus with red faces.

Somebody had left a newspaper in an empty seat. Seymour grabbed it and began tearing the pages. He crumpled them into a ball as they took their seats on the swaying, nearly empty upper deck.

'Here,' he passed the balls of newsprint to Compo. 'You can pad the toes with these.'

It wasn't easy in the space between the seats. Compo grunted and muttered. They took the seat behind and left him to it.

Clegg stared through the window at the dying day. Westwards, cream clouds were buff tinted and the showy hills backlighted with shades of Compo's socks. Bickerdyke's was still open. He was in his doorway nagging at someone inside. They stopped with a swish of air brakes for the pedestrian lights.

I'm going to be a square peg, Clegg was thinking, in a Rainbow Circle.

'Hey up!' Compo said and pointed through the window. In the street to their left, a few yards up the hill, a motorbike and sidecar had stalled. They could see a hat and a weatherproof Wally stamping ineffectively on the kick starter. Through the open roof of the sidecar they caught a glimpse of duck-egg blue. 'She's broken down.'

'I've always thought so,' Seymour agreed, but Compo was

133

gone, clattering down metal stairs. They followed him down before the lights changed, Seymour reluctantly, Clegg glad of a reprieve, however temporary, from the Conjugal Wrights and the risk of inadvertent matrimony.

They tumbled from the moving bus. Compo was halfway to his target already, his feet echoing through the evening street.

'Who does he think he is?' Seymour frowned. 'The R.A.C.?' They moved in pursuit. 'We're going to be late now.'

Hopefully, Clegg silently agreed.

Seething nicely in the sidecar, watching her perspiring spouse getting nowhere very fast, Nora heard what sounded like a horse coming and turned to see what fool could be riding so recklessly.

'Oh God,' she groaned. 'Him! That's all we need.'

He braked as he drew alongside and stood to catch his breath. 'Lucky I just saw thee,' he said.

'I was just thinking the same,' she lied.

'We were on the bus. We nearly went past.'

She sighed.

'Don't fret theeself,' he said, mistaking its import and placing a reassuring hand on her shoulder. She lifted it off, using thumb and forefinger cautiously and was surprised to find it comparatively clean.

'We'll get thee mobile,' he promised. 'Only we shan't have to be long 'cos I've got this bird to meet.' He watched her closely for signs of envy. She hides it well he conceded. But I bet, underneath, she's just gone to jelly.

'I wish you every happiness,' she said.

Well, nearly jelly, he decided.

The sweating Wally was still pumping limply at the kick start. 'What seems to be thee trouble then, Wally?' Compo enquired and then remembered that one of the attributes of Wally's helmet was its ability to insulate him from the world outside. With his head snug inside it he was as good as stone deaf and had been known to wear it in the house when Nora was nagging at him from the kitchen. He was thus still unaware of Compo's arrival. Compo knocked on the helmet.

134

The startled Wally shrieked in alarm. His boot slipped from the kick start and he scraped his ankle painfully. He was still hobbling in agony around the bike when Clegg and Seymour arrived.

'I see you've been helping Wally already,' Clegg said.

'He's a bit of a muffin mechanically,' Compo swung a chalk-striped leg over the saddle. Nora blanched. Whatever, she wondered, is he wearing on his feet? She watched cautiously while Compo exhausted himself on the kick start.

I ought to get out, she decided, but he'd only look at me legs. He always looks at me legs.

She sat tight. The bike coughed wheezily but gave no promise of a start.

'Oh let me,' Seymour scoffed, hauling Compo from the saddle. 'You're framing like a cretin.'

'It's these shoes,' Compo offered in excuse. 'They don't allus go same way as me leg.'

Seymour kicked off magnificently but the bike remained unimpressed.

'Has it got any petrol?' Nora enquired of the now helmetless Wally.

'Of course it's got petrol,' he scoffed. 'What kind of dozy prong's going to . . .' He rapped the tank with his knuckles. It rang disconcertingly hollow. 'They always sound a bit that way,' he explained in a voice full of lack of conviction.

Seymour removed the filler cap, he placed his ear to the tank and shook the machine by the handlebars. There came no sound of liquid swilling in the fumey interior. 'Empty,' he announced.

Wally removed himself hastily from Nora's reach.

They began pushing it towards the nearest pumps. It was uphill but she sat like granite in the sidecar, clutching her handbag, defying anyone to ask her to leave.

Seymour pushed at the handlebars, the others in line abreast at the rear.

'It's good of you to give a bloke a hand,' Wally acknowledged.

'I know,' Clegg gasped.

135

'It's no bother,' Compo said, though the increasing redness of his face testified otherwise.

'Speak for yourself,' Clegg groaned. 'It's marginally better than the Rainbow Circle but only just.'

'I think some beggar must have drained me tank,' Wally offered in excuse.

'Hardly what I had in mind,' Seymour snarled, 'when I put the old dinner jacket on.'

'I hope tha's paying attention, Nora lass,' Compo raised a voice already under stress. 'And observing that there's only me willingly putting me back into this on account of our special relationship.'

'Creeper,' Clegg said.

'A special relationship,' Compo continued, his voice wavering under the strain, 'which I'm sure I'm right in thinking ought to be big enough to stand an occasional misplaced peacock.'

'Just push!' Seymour ordered through gritted teeth.

'He can talk while he's shoving,' Wally protested. 'There's no call for you to start coming between a man and a wife. Especially a man and my wife. Stop interfering.'

Nora gasped and rose wrathfully through the sidecar roof. She began laying about Wally with her handbag. He retreated with the nimble skills of much practice thus setting an example which seemed like an excellent idea to Compo and Clegg who were both under the impression that the avenging handbag was aimed at them.

This abandonment by his crew left Seymour struggling with the weight of the outfit as it threatened to roll back down the hill. A tendency which Nora, with her final swipes, was exacerbating as she swayed and rocked. Seymour made a grab for the hand brake. He yanked it hard and yelped as it trapped his finger painfully. He sucked at the blood blister already forming. They all stared for a moment in mild surprise at the machine as it started backwards down the hill.

Nora felt the change of direction. She clutched the sidecar roof and found herself gathering speed past the imbecile

136

expressions of her husband and his cronies. They were watching her sliding by as if it was some curious impulse on her part which she would stop any second.

She felt like Boadicea reviewing her troops. 'Do something!' she commanded as she glided past.

Galvanised at last into action they did something. They collided as they dashed to halt the machine. Wally went sprawling over an excess of Compo's shoe. Clegg tripped over Wally and went cannoning into Seymour who was just gathering pace in pursuit of the runaway. It was thus Compo who got a headstart to the rescue.

'Hold on, lass,' he ordered as he clattered down the hill. And gamely, en route to disaster, hold on she did – to sidecar, handbag and duck-egg blue hat.

I'm in with a chance here he was thinking as he willed his wayward footwear onwards. I could earn a few points for this one.

A car on its way up the hill mounted the pavement to escape Nora's path. Compo had a glimpse of startled faces as he passed.

The sidecar wheel bounced jarringly from the kerb edge. Nora clung grimly to her hat as the machine careered back across the road. The bump and the detour had slowed it a little and Compo gained a yard or two.

Two thunderstruck female pedestrians scrambled to safety over a low wall. Compo found his attention distracted momentarily by amounts of leg it seemed years since he'd seen.

Recalling himself firmly to the path of duty he made a lunge for the sidecar's nose and managed to grab the sidelight. It suddenly felt as if he was being towed by a train. Off balance now, his legs flying like a signaller's arms, he worked his way into a solid two-handed grip on the little sidelight and began applying maximum braking by slapping both prodigious shoe soles to the floor.

He was rewarded by a not unwelcoming glance from his lady in distress. It wasn't much. She was never flowery but it was the best he'd had all week.

137

He dug his heels in firmer, but there was a lot of weight moving now with a good deal of momentum and he found himself skiing. He could feel the road massaging his feet. It was working slowly. But the crossing was looming and his shoes were getting warmer.

'The hand brake!' he yelled. 'Tha'll have to grab the hand brake.'

Typical, she snorted. They start a job and some woman has to finish it. She began working her way forward towards the handlebars. And where's me husband when all this is happening? Up the damned hill somewhere. Probably worrying about his pigeons.

Down at the junction there was a small tailback from the pedestrian lights. Two cars were trapped in the path of the skier and his reversing lady. Pedestrians were pointing. Faces were glued to vehicle windows. Suddenly the doors of two cars were opened and the occupants fled.

Nora reached the handgrip and squeezed the brake. The machine slowed, then stopped obediently. Which was more than could be said for Compo who found himself sliding up the sidecar's nose, up the incline of its windscreen and into the cockpit to land sprawling on top of the startled Nora. She began struggling vigorously. It was her worst nightmare confirmed. Trapped in a confined space under a ferret fancier.

'Gerroff!' she grunted.

'Steady on!' he pleaded. 'Give us a chance. Stop waving thee elbows about. Tha's reaching parts other elbows seldom reach.'

'Me hat!' she yelped. 'You're crushing me hat.'

'Listen,' he said through gritted teeth in tones of deep sincerity. 'There are worse things being crushed than hats.'

In defence of her dignity she had let go of the brake and they were starting to move again.

The cavalry was coming now, bowling down the hill in the shape of Seymour, legging it strongly on long, dinner-suited legs followed by Clegg at speeds unfamiliar to his best suit and, a long way behind, by an overheated if weatherproof Wally bringing up the rear in his whispering trousers.

138

'They're moving again,' Seymour panted. 'Why is the fool moving again?'

It's just damned inconsiderate, Clegg was thinking.

They could see Compo's legs waving through the roof of the sidecar.

'Fine time,' Clegg gasped, 'to be showing off his new shoes.'

Seymour reached the machine before it had gathered much speed. He caught a glimpse of the seething tangle of limbs in its interior. My God, he shuddered. That's about as close as you can get without being married. He applied the brake.

Clegg came puffing up and helped to hold the machine. They stared in appalled fascination at the gymnastics within.

Seymour tugged at Compo's waving leg. 'You can come out now,' he said.

'I'm trying to flamin' come out,' Compo snarled.

'Get him out!' Nora demanded.

They manoeuvred the machine until its wheel was safely locked against the kerb. Joined now by old Whispering Trousers who, despite his purple face and hothouse temperature, seemed intrigued by the unusual views he kept glimpsing of his wife, they all three took handfuls of the writhing chalk-stripe and plucked Compo from the sidecar depths. He came free with flushed face and certain powerful memories of his recent experiences.

'She's all woman is Nora. I could never abandon that for a Mrs Jack Halliwell. I'd have hated having to call a bird Jack anyway.'

They assisted Nora from the sidecar. The duck-egg blue hat was way down over one ear but it was her skirt she was plucking at in embarrassment as she stepped into the roadway.

Her entrance was greeted by applause and a burst of cheering and they all became uncomfortably aware of the grinning spectators at the junction.

Knowing what was coming, Wally sought the security of his helmet. Hot as he was he burrowed in there and thus was insulated from the details, if not the import, of what the

139

furious Nora began dishing out verbally as she preened the feathers of her battered hat.

She began walking home. Dinner was off.

Petrol obtained, Wally gave them a lift to the Three Legs. The bar was quiet. They sat quietly at a table.

'Well,' Wally sighed gloomily and announced for the third time, 'I suppose I ought to be getting home.' He got no reply and he made no move.

Their glasses empty, Clegg collected them and went for another round.

'Enjoying a night out?' the landlord enquired sarcastically with a nod at the three miserable faces at the table. Clegg took the drinks back and made a fourth.

Clegg raised his glass. 'Happy birthday, Nora.'

'She'll kill me,' Wally prophesied. 'She was looking forward to going out for a meal.'

'All right, so she's missed a meal. But if she looks on the bright side she's still got me. I haven't run off wi' a Mrs Jack Halliwell.'

'It's all right for some,' Wally said. 'Who only see her on a part-time basis. It's me what has to go home and face her.'

'Listen,' Compo said. 'For a while there in that sidecar there was nobody facing her closer than me.'

'What really peeves me,' Seymour glared at Wally, 'is how much grease I've managed to get on my dinner jacket from your damned machine.'

'A bloke has to keep his machine in good lubricated condition,' Wally protested.

'No petrol,' Seymour appealed to his audience. 'Just smothered in grease.'

'Like the meal,' Clegg said. 'If you'd gone to some Italian place.'

'That's true,' Compo agreed. 'That's a line tha could take. Explain to her that between us we've probably saved her from a night of horrible heartburn.'

140

'We weren't going to any Italian place.'

'Oh well, if tha's going to be difficult about it.'

They went back to silence. The darts team were practising in the corner.

They might have been the arrows of Cupid, Seymour reflected. Suppose Mrs Exactly Right was waiting for me at the Rainbow Circle. With a modest private income. He sipped his drink. Not too modest.

'I'll have to be getting home,' Wally said, but remained seated.

Another pint later, Wally followed up with a further announcement. 'I daren't go home,' he said.

They regarded him sympathetically. It came as no surprise.

'Tha can doss down at my place,' Compo offered. 'For one night.'

'One night's no good. I daren't go home ever.'

They regarded him with more interest. He was obviously flirting with larger ideas than they'd suspected. Under the influence of their third pints and these revolutionary new Wally possibilities their depression was lifting.

'What's tha going to do then, Wal?'

'I'm thinking,' Wally said.

'A new life. Well why not?' Seymour approved. 'It's not as if there's any children.'

'I don't know why we never had children,' Wally reflected. 'I mean I know why for the last thirty years – but in the beginning.'

'You could use that as the excuse when it gets into solicitor's hands,' Clegg suggested. 'No children. After forty years they can't say you haven't been patient. But finally. Reluctantly. You feel compelled to go off and start a family before it's too late.'

They studied the diminutive Wally still in his weather-proofs but now under the new aura Clegg had just invested him with as potential father of his race.

'I think it is too late,' Compo sniffed.

'And if it's not now it will be by the time he gets all that damned gear off,' Seymour scoffed.

141

'Solicitor's hands?' Wally looked worried.

'Well, if you're determined you're never going home again. Permanently.'

'I'm determined,' Wally shuddered. 'Permanently. She's going to be totally unlivable with after what happened to her best hat. And on her birthday an' all,' he added gloomily.

'It was Twinkletoes here who crushed the hat,' Seymour pointed out.

'Tha should a seen what she were crushing,' Compo protested.

'But it were me that ran out a petrol,' Wally insisted. 'The husband. When they've had a spot of bother and they're looking to give somebody some anguish for it – it's always the husband.'

They couldn't argue with that.

'Still,' Wally added. 'If it gets into solicitor's hands I don't know as I'd want to stand up in court and say I'd walked out on account of having no kids.'

Seymour snorted. 'Well they won't grant you a separation on the grounds that you daren't go home.'

'It seems damned unfair,' Wally sighed. 'I can't think of a better reason.'

'Anyway what would you do at your age,' Clegg enquired, 'suddenly on your own?'

'I presume you mean apart from enjoying it,' Wally said. 'There must be a hundred things a bloke could do.'

'After a broken romance,' Seymour chuckled, 'it's customary to join the French Foreign Legion.'

'They'd fail him on his height,' Compo cackled.

Clegg finished his drink. 'It's time we took him home.'

'No,' Wally backed in alarm. 'I like the Foreign Legion idea better.'

They called for an Indian Take Away. They called at Bickerdyke's for a bottle of wine. He blew the dust off it. 'Whose birthday is it?'

142

They pointed to Wally. 'It's his missis.'

'Shouldn't spoil 'em,' Bickerdyke said, tacking 5p extra on the price as a Stupidity Tax.

They pushed Wally in his whispering trousers up his front steps, his arms laden with Chicken Tandoori and Vegetable Curry, the wine in the pocket of his motoring coat.

It's true, Clegg was thinking, he looks like a seasoned old Japanese campaigner.

'Don't leave me,' Wally pleaded.

'Get off home,' Compo said.

'Ring the bell,' ordered Seymour. 'Shower her with your gifts. Have a good birthday supper.'

'I feel I ought to be wearing me helmet,' Wally hesitated at his door.

'Ring the bell,' they chorused and withdrew into the shadows.

They watched him ring gingerly. The light came on in the hall. They held their breath. The door opened. In the light from the hallway they saw him squeezing his features into an unconvincing smile.

'Happy bir—' he said before a hand emerged from the doorway and yanked him in. They heard the door close.

'Did tha see that?' Compo breathed, his voice replete with admiration. 'I bet Mrs Jack Halliwell wouldn't have had a grip like that.'

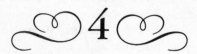

Howard was out early. Thoroughly cleaning the chip van parked outside the house. Before the sun had any warmth he was sweating, getting in all the corners, inside and out. Everybody's vehicle would be gleaming today. Trade would be brisk. Expansive, large, festive appetites on parade today at the gala field.

Pearl was helping. Her hot water steaming. Bringing the fryers back to a high gloss. Burnishing the surfaces. Checking for traces of the other woman. Alert for hairpins, lipstick, nail varnish.

Howard was guiltily aware of this sub-theme of his wife's activity. He had done his own safety check before she arrived, but he knew from prickly experience how fallible was the masculine vision by comparison with the questing female eye. He was praying quietly now for a bonus from the gods of gala days and errant husbands.

Clegg opened his front door and reached for his milk bottle. He felt socially lightweight in slippers and braces in the teeth of all the chip-van activity and withdrew quickly with his bottle.

His kettle was whistling. He warmed the pot. Boiled up again and this time mashed the tea. His back door was wide open to the already sunny garden. He poured the cream from

144

the milk into a saucer and took it outside for the brindle cat which visited him every morning. It was waiting for him on a fencepost, pretending indifference, its coat sleek – well-nourished, not at all a stray. He liked its splendid self-assurance.

'Morning,' he said.

The cat continued to pretend to ignore him as he knew it would. He went back inside to pour his tea. He returned with his cup to the garden. The cat and the cream were gone. He smiled and did his morning's tour of his tiny flowerbeds. Chatting amiably, between sips of his tea, to a plodding beetle, to a harassed bee, and admiring the silent small engine that was powering the blur of fragile wing which was holding a hoverfly steady in that particle of infinity which began just above his antirrhinums.

They cycled to Seymour's. Clegg wincing at the falsetto squeak from Compo's rusty machine.

'How long's that been going on?'

'How long's what been going on?' Compo asked in genuine puzzlement.

Clegg sighed. 'Long enough to drive you selectively deaf apparently. Your bicycle's shrieking in pain.'

'Oh that,' Compo snorted dismissively. 'Tha'll get used to it.'

'When we get to Seymour's,' Clegg threatened, 'I'm going to put some oil on it.'

'Fusspot,' Compo said.

There was a breeze as they pedalled high on the moors but the day was warming up. Every road junction had a sign pointing the way to the gala. It was too early yet for the anticipated traffic.

They propped their bikes against Seymour's wall. Compo moved briskly to be the first to get his finger on the button of

145

Seymour's home-made entry phone, a device whose unreliable vagaries Compo found fascinating.

A tinny squawk from the instrument was, as usual, indecipherable, but was plainly not pleased with the vigour with which Compo was button-pressing.

'Come again,' Compo demanded of the phone.

It came again but wasn't any clearer.

'Open the fizzin' door,' Compo suggested forcefully.

They heard the instrument buzz but no sound of movement from the door latch. Compo rattled the door knob. The door remained firmly closed.

They went round the back and banged on Seymour's rear door. He opened it frustratedly. 'Just a minute,' he ordered. 'There's someone at the front door.' He closed the door in their faces before they could explain. They exchanged a glance and rolled their eyes and waited. Seymour re-opened the door a trifle sheepishly. 'Why didn't you tell me it was you?'

'It's a good bloke,' Compo said, 'who can tell thee anything.'

Seymour was in his working smock. The garment which Compo was in the habit of referring to, derisively, as 'Seymour's Inventor's Pinny.' 'Tea in the pot,' he said.

They poured themselves a beaker. As they turned with these Seymour thrust plates into their free hands. 'A slice of Edie's famous cherry cake.' He offered the cake plate enticingly.

Their impulse to reach for a slab was frustrated by their already full hands. Seymour made no attempt to ease their predicament but stood smirking as he watched them balancing their plates on their beakers in order to free a hand.

'Exactly,' he nodded, removing the cake plate from their reach. 'Difficult, isn't it?'

'Chuffin' impossible if tha's going to keep moving it,' a cakeless Compo complained.

'The infernal balancing act with food and drink while standing,' Seymour explained. 'Never enough hands. The human body badly designed for vertical picnicking purposes. You'll see it today at the gala. Poor devils struggling with

146

scalding tea and soggy sandwiches. One of the oldest problems of civilised man. And one to which there has thus far been no satisfactory solution – until – ' Seymour produced with a flourish what looked like a plastic bib. He hung it round Clegg's neck.

'What is it?' Clegg backed away suspiciously.

'What it is,' Seymour hauled Clegg back into range again, 'is the Utterthwaite Picnicker's Friend. The essential aid to al fresco snacks. A small, portable personal table.' He demonstrated the utility of the device by raising and clicking into place the spring-loaded, half-circular, foldaway leaf of the thing which was now sticking out from Clegg's middle regions and onto which Seymour now encouraged him to stand his beaker and his plate.

'There you are, you see,' the proud inventor waved a creator's paternal hand. 'With the aid of the Utterthwaite Picnicker's Friend, I have restored to the human species, when eating outdoors, the unrestricted use of both its hands.'

Clegg stared at the little platform about his navel.

'Came to me in a moment of inspiration,' Seymour explained. 'Trouble is it came a bit late. It's a question of how many can we produce in time for the gala.'

There was a crash as Clegg's navel platform collapsed spilling the beaker and its contents down his leg. He began to hop in sudden activity, plucking hot trouser from his legs.

'I think perhaps Mark Two should be a trifle sturdier,' Seymour admitted.

Compo put his beaker down and helped himself to a piece of cake.

They were cycling back to town now, heading for Wesley's. In times of manufacturing need, when looking for some muffin to do the actual work, Seymour invariably headed for his brother-in-law.

'A relationship whose few advantages I may as well utilise,' Seymour was inclined to pronounce.

Besides, it was always nice to see Edie who doted on her

147

brother Seymour whom, despite all the evidence, she continued to regard as the brains of the family.

'Drains is closer,' Wesley once said and suffered a bitter season thereafter in his marital calendar.

He groaned now deep in the darkest recesses of his garden shed as he saw his brother-in-law arriving with Compo and Clegg.

'No,' Wesley said firmly, looking with some scepticism at the Picnicker's Friend, Mark One.

'Something a bit more solid,' his brother-in-law patted Wesley encouragingly, if cautiously, on a diesel-stained boiler-suited shoulder.

'Something a lot more solid,' Clegg said, shaking a damp leg.

'If you wanted 'em for gala day, why didn't you ask me sooner?'

'It's only last night I had the inspiration.'

Wesley sighed.

'If you could quickly knock us together perhaps twenty,' Seymour was calculating. 'It's not as many as I would like but we can keep re-hiring those twenty over and over again. There should be a very good profit ratio on these if they're handled properly.'

'I don't want you to think I'm not grateful,' Clegg said, 'for getting tea all down me leg but I have to point out that it left me with the distinct impression that the damn things don't work.'

'Don't work? Don't work?' Seymour's head rose dangerously near the roof of the shed as he gathered up his inventor's dignity.

'It's just an impression,' the chastened Clegg said.

'It's one of thee better impressions,' Compo confirmed.

'Of course they'll work. And I'll thank you not to go around spreading irresponsible and malicious rumours. It's whispers like that which can undermine people's confidence in a new product.'

'Sorry,' Clegg said.

'Admittedly,' Seymour conceded, 'when tested operationally we discovered the need for a minor modification to the prototype. But that's what prototypes are for. To be tested to the limit in order to reveal any flaw.'

'It was all over the floor,' Clegg said. 'One cup of tea. That's really testing to the limits.'

'It worked, didn't it?' Seymour insisted. 'I was able to identify where the problem was and now' – he patted Wesley's shoulder cautiously again – 'we can make sure that the first batch of twenty Mark Two are up to the standard the public will come to expect of an Utterthwaite product.'

'I can't make twenty by dinner time,' Wesley protested. 'I've got to get ready for the gala too, you know.'

'They're very simple.' Seymour smiled complacently. 'The best inventions always are.'

From inside the house, Edie was watching the shed, only half-listening to the young married chatter of her daughter Glenda, dropped in for a coffee and to discuss their family itinerary for the gala.

'I saw some in Pendlebury's reduced.'

'Your Uncle Seymour's spending a lot of time these days in funny company.'

'Actually I think I'd prefer something with a fleck in it.'

'Norman Clegg's presentable at a push. He merely looks a bit retarded, but the other one!' She made a few disapproving clucking sounds. 'I expect Our Seymour regards it as his duty to improve them educationally.' She turned away from the window. 'My God, he must like a challenge!'

'What are you doing with the best cups, mother? We'll have a beaker.'

'It's not for us, love. It's just in case your Uncle Seymour would care for a coffee. He's used to the best, your Uncle Seymour.'

'Because you're always spoiling him.'

'We always have, love. He was the only boy among all us girls.' She polished the fine, bone china lovingly, withdrawn

149

into childhood memories. 'And the brains of the family.'

Glenda sighed. 'It's me dad he comes running to whenever there's a job to be done.'

'Your father's good with his hands. You know he's only happy when he's hammering.'

'And I hope he hasn't come with a last-minute job for me dad this morning. It'll soon be time to get him ready for the gala.'

'Your Uncle Seymour knows what he's doing. He wouldn't be coming here on gala day to commandeer your father.'

They heard the clatter of Wesley's old Land Rover starting up. They got to the window in time to see it chugging into the street.

'I told you,' Glenda said.

They rode and bounced in Wesley's Land Rover as far as Arnold's Scrapyard. Rank Arnold detached himself from a pile of rusting motor bodies and came to meet them, wiping filthy hands on his filthy overall.

'You'll have to be quick,' Rank Arnold announced. 'I'm closing early for gala day.'

'No you're not!' A shrill voice startled them as it came like a high-speed drill from the living-van behind them. They saw Rank Arnold's bird glowering in the caravan doorway. Britannia of a sea of decrepit metal. Size 20 biceps bulging from an 18 dress. Twenty years younger than Arnold and twice as rough.

'You can stay here. You're not making a fool outa me. Getting stinko and over-friendly with your wife.'

'That's a lie,' Arnold protested. 'I've never been over-friendly with the wife.'

'And you're not going to be today. Or tonight. You just let me catch you anywhere near that gala.' She glared at them all savagely as if defying any answer before withdrawing into the van and slamming the flimsy door.

Rank Arnold removed his greasy trilby and passed a filthy

150

hand through his thinning hair. 'Like I was saying. Take your time,' he sighed.

'Not going to the gala then, Arnold,' Compo said.

'What gala?' Arnold shrugged.

They fell in step and walked with him between the metal mountains.

'Tha dropped a bit of a goolie shacking up wi' that one, Arnold,' Compo sympathised.

'She int allus like that,' Arnold explained. 'That's only when she's sober. Get some ale down her and she becomes really unpleasant.'

They exchanged truly impressed glances.

'Trouble is,' Arnold continued, 'there's practically nowhere you can flaming hide in a caravan.' He waved a stained arm expansively over his corroding kingdom. 'I spend many a night out here. I've made meself tolerably comfy in the back of an old Humber.'

'A man should be master in his own house,' Seymour pronounced. He found them all staring at him as if they were visitors and he was confined in some asylum.

'Where's his missis, then?' Arnold enquired of Compo.

'Left him,' Compo chuckled.

Arnold nodded unsurprised.

'It's me brother-in-law,' Wesley made the introduction.

'Can't win 'em all,' Arnold sympathised.

They explained their errand and Arnold led them to a shed where he stored his offcuts of hardboard, plywood and plastic. 'What's it for?' he enquired as he watched Seymour rifling through the oddments of sheet plastic.

Seymour leapt smartly to clap a hand over Compo's mouth as he was about to answer. Seymour smiled falsely at Arnold. 'Spot of model making.'

'Be like that,' Rank Arnold said.

By mid-morning, traffic was building. The tents were up in the gala field.

151

Lorries with gleaming paintwork were being transformed into floats for the big parade.

The Reverend Charles Bean-Peach was assembling his troops in the church hall for the historical pageant. His inspiration everywhere leaving a trail of Christian resentment.

Amid his favourite acoustics in the Staff Only toilet at the Town Hall, the mayor was practising his secretary's speech.

Marina was applying eye-liner at her dressing-table mirror.

The Polaroid Kid in his tea break at City Office Equipment was browsing through his library copy of *How to Photograph the Female Form*.

The brothers Wilkinson were still in bed.

Wesley was swearing steadily in his shed as he assembled, under Seymour's directions, the seventh Utterthwaite Picnicker's Friend.

Clegg and Compo were at their duties on that same assembly line.

Bickerdyke's were offering Giant Gala Balloons.

Wally was polishing his best squeaky boots.

Nora was ironing his shirt with forceful strokes, determined that the Batty linen would be of the crispest.

At the gala field they were carrying crates into the beer tent.

The Conjugal Wrights were supervising the finishing touches to the float which, in the big parade, would carry a hand-picked selection from the Rainbow Circle.

Nora locked her front door and tried the handle vigorously. Wally creaked down the steps in his squeaky boots. Compo appeared in his best chalk stripe, his hair plastered with solid brilliantine, and gasped with admiration at Nora's best going-to-bingo smooth, unwrinkled legs. 'I'll see thee at the gala, lass,' he winked broadly.

'Not if I see you first,' she stuck her nose in the air and

departed at a furious pace pursued without enthusiasm by the squeaky boots.

'I'll save thee a Picnicker's Friend,' Compo volunteered as Nora turned the corner.

'Filth,' she announced to the squeaky boots. 'He's always talking filth.'

The gala was already in high gear when they paid their entrance money. Seymour and Clegg stood resolutely by while Compo delved through the unfamiliar pockets of his racy chalk stripe in search of coin. The man with the tickets sighed. 'It's here somewhere,' Compo promised. They watched him dig deep into the abundance of new trousers and set their faces stonily against any impulse to offer him charity. It was far too early in the day to be falling for his financial gymnastics.

'But you have to admire the way he tries,' Clegg conceded.

'Very often at times like this,' Compo reminded them, 'a bloke's mates will buy a ticket for him and he can pay 'em back later.'

'How about that?' the ticket man looked at Seymour and Clegg hopefully.

They moved on their way.

'Never seen him before,' Clegg said. 'We thought he was with you.'

'Hey up,' Compo complained to their disappearing backs as he produced his money for the ticket. 'I hope tha's not going to take this as some sort of precedent.'

He caught up with them. They were carrying between them, twenty-two Picnicker's Friends. They walked past the pony jumping. The town band was playing in midfield, its light classical selection in conflict with the sound-track from the fairground's whirligig machines.

'Hang on to these,' Compo thrust his plastic devices towards their inventor. 'While I have a go on the dodgems.'

'Later,' Seymour ordered.

153

'I have to go later as well. I always start wi' a go on the dodgems. Gets me in the proper gala mood.'

Seymour hauled Compo back to the path of duty. A chunk of chalk stripe in Seymour's grip, Compo found himself being propelled towards the Refreshment Tent. 'When has he ever,' Seymour rolled his eyes at Clegg, 'not been in a gala mood? He's spent his entire life in a gala mood. What has he ever done with life except fritter it away?'

'Tell him,' Clegg nudged Compo.

'Its true,' Compo admitted. 'I've had a good fritter.'

'What has he ever done as a contribution towards existence?'

'Tell him,' Clegg urged.

'Pass,' Compo said.

Seymour halted them before the Refreshment Tent. There was a small queue. People were emerging with expressions of agony from the burning bite of hot plastic cups as they juggled with things on paper plates. Seymour smiled. 'Our customers await.' He gathered his little sales force for its final briefing.

Edie sat resplendent in gala finery in the car waiting for Wesley to come out of the house. Glenda shuffled impatiently in the back seat alongside her husband Barry.

'What's me dad doing?'

'He's nearly ready.' Edie tightened her grip on her handbag defensively, preparing to repel the accusations against her brother Seymour.

'He could have been ready hours ago if he hadn't been ambushed by me Uncle Seymour.'

The placid Barry stirred uneasily. He hated being caught in a combat zone.

'Your Uncle Seymour,' Edie retaliated in her best capo di monte voice, 'knows what he's doing.'

'Every time,' Glenda agreed. 'He gets me dad to do it.'

Barry gazed longingly out of his window at a summer sky above the chimneys of Ackroyd Street.

154

'You should be happy Our Glenda that your Uncle Seymour gives his tame to wadening your father's horazons. Left to his own devices your father would spend his entire life living under a jacked-up motor car.'

'He's very good with motor cars.'

'You can have too much of a good thing.' Edie gave the horn a commanding toot. 'The most I usually see of your father is a pair of boots. I've spent years of my married life having to carry on a conversation with little more than his feet.'

Wesley came out of the house ill at ease in his unaccustomed suit.

'It's supposed to be a holiday. I don't know why a bloke can't go dressed casually. In a pair of overalls.' He caught the full flavour of Edie's glare. 'A pair of clean, neatly pressed overalls,' he amended hastily.

The glare remained unsoftened. 'Now go back and lock the door, you great muffin.'

He smiled sheepishly and hurried back up the path. Edie sighed.

Barry glanced at his wife from the corner of his eye. She's quite a bit like her mother, he was thinking. A reliable, firm breed. Decision makers. He settled back in his corner with a warm feeling of security.

After half an hour's three-pronged sales drive about the precincts of the Refreshment Tent when they counted up they discovered that of their original twenty-two Picnicker's Friends they now had exactly twenty-two.

'You're not trying,' Seymour accused.

'What about thee?' Compo enquired, not unreasonably. 'Tha's not got rid of any either.'

'I tend to intimidate people,' Seymour confessed modestly. 'It's my headmasterly bearing. It overawes them. They scurry away. Fearful they might let something slip ungrammatically.'

'A few I tried let slip ungrammatically,' Compo confirmed.

155

'Tha should have heard what they were saying about thee Picnicker's Friend.'

'Most of mine laughed,' Clegg said. 'You show 'em your Picnicker's Friend and they start to giggle.'

They watched the temperamental inventor kicking viciously at the litter of paper cups on the grass. 'Ingrates,' he snarled. 'I bet it was just the same when some genius invented the wheel. Hello, they said, here comes the idiot with his wheel. Try not to look at him. It only encourages him.'

They watched Seymour struggling to regain control of his errant temper. He returned to them wearing an unconvincing smile. 'Mustn't be discouraged.' He clapped them on the back.

'If it's all the same to you,' Clegg said, 'I really feel like being discouraged.'

'I'm going on the dodgems,' Compo announced.

Seymour stepped in smartly to quell the incipient mutiny. 'It'll be different this time,' he promised. 'There's always a bit of resistance at first to something new. What we need is a good demonstration.' He reached for Clegg but Clegg had gone.

'I'm not in the market,' Clegg was muttering, 'for another wet leg.'

'That was the earlier model,' Seymour hissed in a suppressed whisper. 'And kindly keep your voice down. No point in deliberately undermining the confidence of potential clients.' He smiled unconvincingly at the small crowd around the entrance to the Refreshment Tent.

The marketing elements behind his smile were wasted since the crowd's attention, to a man, was focused on the much more fascinating spectacle of Compo almost lost in the depths of his chalk-striped suit. For the greater comfort of gala-day feet he was back in his white-painted trainers and the effect was striking.

Munching their refreshments his spectators were entranced. 'What is he?' a sausage roll asked.

'He's overdressed, that's what he is,' a ham sandwich mumbled with feeling.

156

'He must be one of the turns,' a pork pie suggested.

'Don't stare,' the pork pie's wife said. 'He may just be retarded.'

They watched Seymour quell Compo's objections and begin fitting him with a Picnicker's Friend.

'Told you,' the pork pie's wife said. 'That's his attendant making sure he's wearing his bib.'

As Seymour led the reluctant Compo into the tent the pork pie's wife followed. She pushed in front of Clegg and thrust a pound coin into Compo's hand. 'Here you are, love,' she said. 'Enjoy the gala in your own simple way.'

'Oh ta,' Compo grinned and pinched her broad bottom in his own simple way. She gasped. The pork pie saw his wife returning, her face scarlet. 'What's the matter?' he asked.

She stuck her nose in the air and began leading him away. 'He's not as slow as you think.'

After two goes on the bingo, Ivy and Nora were heading for the Refreshment Tent. Ivy was splendid in her best hat. Nora, feeling shabby in her second best, was still spitting feathers mentally at the moulting of her best duck-egg blue. Then some niggling instinct brought her senses to the alert. Some familiar note was missing from the gala sounds around her. The squeaky boots!

She turned to see Wally lagging far behind. She beckoned him onwards. He sighed and quickened his pace. It was never any surprise to me, he told himself, that the British were the first to discover radar.

The two women waited for him. Ultra-sensitive, marital ears detected the rebellious note in the squeak of his boots.

'Don't start,' she said.

'Start what?' he protested.

'You know what. Not on gala day.'

'I don't know what.'

'You do know what.'

'Are we going for a cuppa tea or aren't we?' Ivy enquired.

157

'We are when he stops being so wilful.' Nora glared a force nine at Wally.

'You go and get a cuppa,' he suggested. 'I thought I might have a stroll to the beer tent.'

'You see,' Nora said. 'Wilful.' She gave him a shove towards the Refreshment Tent. 'You can have a cuppa tea like the rest of us.'

'I'll have a cuppa tea,' Wally conceded. 'Like the rest of you.'

They went towards the tent. 'I should think so,' Nora settled her second-best hat. 'There's time enough to be starting on beer. You've got all the day still before you.'

'No need to rub it in.'

'What was that? What was that you said?'

'I said will it have sugar in,' Wally improvised nimbly. Ivy gave him a look which announced that he wasn't fooling her.

'Of course it'll have sugar in,' Nora said, 'if you want sugar in. It'll do you more good than beer. And you can have a sandwich or something. Get some food down before you start swilling ale.' They were entering the tent. 'Eeh,' she confided to Ivy. 'They can't wait to start swilling ale.'

Compo spotted her as she came in. His old, badly-shaven face lit up with a grin. He moved towards her, awkwardly balancing three cups of tea on the little platform hanging round his middle.

'Where's he going with our tea?' Clegg enquired.

'It doesn't matter,' Seymour decided. 'Leave him be. Let him demonstrate to people how much freedom and mobility are retained while wearing the Picnicker's Friend.'

They watched him tiptoeing crablike between the groups in the warm, underwater-like, canvas interior, his face now showing frustration at the limits on his speed imposed by the storms growing in the three teacups. He was eager to intercept Nora before she reached the counter. To surprise her with the first of his peace offerings for gala day, the gift of three teas and perhaps the promise of a bacon sarni should she fancy it. What the hell! It was a day for large gestures. To begin to mend the misunderstandings of what had been a tricky week.

158

Him and his fizzin Picnicker's Friend! A bloke can't move faster than a fossil wearing one of these things. And if I take it off I'm going to spill everything.

By trial and error he had discovered the best compromise between forward motion and the steadying of his little platform. Unfortunately the result was a knees-bent waddle which felt ridiculous even to him and was causing considerable amusement to sundry spectators.

Though not to Seymour. 'Why is he walking like that?' Seymour groaned.

'There are some things,' Clegg said, 'into which I think it's never wise to pry.'

'He should be smiling. Making it look easy.'

'If you wanted him to go modelling your wares I think you should have started him gradually. Had him walking round with a book on his head.'

'I'd love,' Seymour muttered through clenched teeth, 'to lay a book on his head.'

Nora was nearing the counter. She heard the call from behind her. 'Nora, lass.' She winced at the unmistakable tones.

'Don't look. You'll encourage him,' she spun Wally back on course and kept her own back resolutely turned. Ivy glanced over her shoulder. Compo waved which was a mistake that deposited three cups of tea in his lap.

At the sound of him whinnying like a horse the tent fell silent. All eyes, including Nora's, swivelled to the source. He was walking in that hallowed tradition of all men with wet trousers.

Nora averted her eyes as he began plucking at them. It's the last thing you want to see, she decided, in a Refreshment Tent.

Ivy was using a daintily inadequate hanky to suppress her giggles. Wally was grinning broadly. Seymour alone of all the male spectators seemed impervious to the knockabout charm of Compo's footwork. He strode forward boldly to interrupt the dance. He took a hold on Compo's chalk striped collar.

'What kind of demonstration is that, you fool?'

The spectators were further enlivened by the sight of a

159

furious Compo removing his Picnicker's Friend to use it as a weapon as he pursued a startled Seymour from the tent. Their rapid exit, in the best traditions of Yorkshire sportsmanship, was accompanied by a round of spontaneous applause.

'I was in with a chance there,' Compo was complaining bitterly as he shifted uneasily in his soggy trousers in the back of Wesley's car. Barry was driving. Wesley having been forbidden by his womenfolk from disappearing yet again on Seymour duty. 'I could have started improving me frosty relations wi' Nora. It's been a bad week,' Compo moaned. 'She's going to think I'm wild and unreliable.'

'Good grief man,' Seymour snorted. 'I wonder where she could possibly get that idea?'

'I've tried. Tha knows I've tried but everything's gone wrong. I thought I'd nip in there – well dressed – wi' three cups a' tea and we'd be away again. And even that went wrong.' He plucked gloomily at the soggy material around his crutch.

'Where to?' Barry enquired.

'To my place,' Seymour instructed. 'Where we shall dry and press his trousers and have him back at the gala in no time. Good as new.'

'Better would be better,' Clegg said.

'It's not funny,' Compo shuffled squelchily. 'Tha's not got to sit in these damn things. And neither have I,' he announced with sudden resolution as he began peeling off the clammy garments.

'What are you doing, man?' Seymour protested. 'You can't take them off in here.'

'In the back seat of a car?' Compo scoffed, unrepentant. 'I'd like a bob for every pair that's ever been off in the back seat of a car.'

Seymour and Clegg sought to evade the sight as Compo got to his feet in the swaying car.

'Sit down,' Seymour ordered. 'Barry can't see through the rear-view mirror.'

160

'It's all right,' Barry said hastily. 'At the moment I don't think I want to see through the rear-view mirror.'

Compo kicked his legs free from the trousers and resumed his seat between Seymour and Clegg who tried to avert their eyes from the excesses of Compo's cloudy grey underwear.

The very stuff, Clegg shuddered, if ever you needed something for wrapping dead ferrets in.

Barry slowed for a junction. There were gala-bound pedestrians on both pavements. Seymour prayed fervently that no one would look in. He began to breathe again as the car turned and picked up speed. Most of the traffic was heading for the gala field.

'It's no good,' Compo squirmed. 'Me Long Johns are soggy as well.'

'No!' Seymour and Clegg panicked simultaneously and clamped Compo firmly down in his seat. 'You're not removing those.'

'Hey up,' he said. 'I was only going to shuffle me bottom a bit.'

'Leave it where it is,' Seymour commanded.

'Think dry thoughts,' Clegg suggested.

'It's all right for thee,' Compo accused and fought his way free. Their resistance was hampered by a certain natural delicacy. In their struggle to hold him there were parts of him on offer which were best left alone. He was thus able to clamber his way across Clegg to the window.

'Get him off,' Clegg pleaded. 'It's not natural under here.'

Compo wound down the window and jammed his rear end into the slipstream. He sighed with relief. 'That's better,' he said. 'Get a bit a' breeze round it.'

'Will you wind that window up!' the horrified Seymour ordered.

'That could be nasty,' Compo frowned.

P.C. Two Four Nine on gala duty directing traffic waved their car onwards. Clegg saw him blink as they passed.

P.C. Two Four Nine shook his head to clear it of residual images. It's been a weird week, he decided. First the headless hostage and now – that. Sticking out of a window. He

161

shuddered. The last thing you'd expect to see with a frame round it.

They drove to Seymour's. He led them into his workshop. He had an old spin-drier linked to a bicycle frame. Handling Compo's trousers somewhat fastidiously he dropped them into the drier.

'What is it?' Compo enquired.

'What does it look like?' the offended Seymour snorted.

'It looks like no place to be stuffin' anybody's trousers in.'

'You're looking at the world's first, fully practical, Low Tech Clothes Drier,' Seymour announced and waited confidently for noises of approval and admiration.

It seemed suddenly very quiet. A fly was buzzing in the grimy windowpane. Clegg felt embarrassed for Seymour and strove to come up with something appreciative. 'Fancy,' he mumbled. 'Wow! You don't see many of – I like it – we all like it.' He nudged Barry and Compo.

'Great,' Barry said.

'Imagine,' Clegg said giving the unimpressed Compo another dig. 'A Low Tech Clothes Drier.'

'It's terrible,' Compo announced loudly. 'It's like a piece a junk from Rank Arnold's.'

'This isn't the final design package,' Seymour protested. 'I haven't had time, as yet, to worry about the appearance.'

'And it shows,' Compo said.

'The first priority,' Seymour snarled, 'is to get the engineering right. I'm thinking of going very heavily into Low Tech. It's a plus for energy conservation and there is, of course, a very clear Third World application.'

'A what?' Compo looked to Clegg.

'He means,' Clegg explained. 'That unelectrified Africa is waiting desperately for a bicycle-powered Low Tech Clothes Drier.'

'Precisely,' Seymour patted his machine.

162

'What's wrong wi' the sun?' Compo asked.

'Don't over-excite your brain,' Seymour warned. 'With technical matters beyond your competence.

'I'm asking,' Compo insisted. 'What's wrong wi' the sun?'

Seymour took a turn around his workshop, teeth clenched. They watched him stamp viciously on an empty gallon-can. 'What about all those who do their washing at night?' He booted the can across the floor. Recovering a measure of control he returned and ordered Compo into the saddle of the bicycle frame. 'All right. Start pedalling.'

'Why me?'

'They're your trousers dammit.' He hoisted Compo in his Long Johns saddlewards. 'Besides which, the act of pedalling will help dry your underpants.'

Compo sat clammily on the bicycle seat. 'Why don't I pop me Long Johns in the drier as well?'

Objections rose instantly. Seymour's the most explicit. 'I could never,' he told Compo with great depth of feeling, 'permit you to sit on any invention of mine in that condition.'

Compo began pedalling. 'Faster,' Seymour instructed. Compo began pedalling faster. 'Faster,' Seymour repeated.

'Rotten hell!' Compo protested.

'Save your breath,' Seymour suggested. He turned his attention to Barry and Clegg. 'It's really very simple.' He patted the drier.

'For some,' Compo gasped.

'The interior is ingenious,' Seymour was waxing eloquent for the benefit of Clegg and Barry who were more interested in Compo's Long Johns under stress. 'I'm using parts cannibalised from a domestic hair drier. Faster!' he urged his captive cyclist.

Compo found enough wind for a raspberry.

'The action of pedalling,' Seymour continued, 'provides sufficient power to heat the element and activate the small fan.'

That's not a bad description of Compo, Clegg decided. With his obsession for Nora Batty. A small fan. And the way his legs are going he's certainly activated.

163

'I think I've had enough,' Compo said. Seymour ignored the plaintive voice.

'I've had enough,' Compo gasped. 'If I carry on pedalling at this rate, me Long Johns are going to start smoking from the friction.'

'They are smoking,' Barry said. But it wasn't the Long Johns. It was the machine.

'They can't possibly be dry yet,' Seymour said confidently, his back to the machine.

'What I can't understand,' Clegg sounded apologetic, 'is why – if they're not done yet – have they started smoking?'

Seymour spun round to check his equipment. 'Oh my God! Stop pedalling!' he ordered the confused Compo to whom all things had become a blur. Then he realised it wasn't blur. It was smoke.

'Me bags!' He tottered wearily from the saddle. 'Me best bags!'

Clegg would long remember the pitiful wail as Compo saw his dreams of a Gala Night Dance with Nora going up in sooty matter.

'There's a fire in me best bags.'

At Seymour's command Barry was driving them towards Rank Arnold's. Seymour was riding in front with Barry, keeping as much distance as possible between himself and the desolate figure in Long Johns who was staring into the future bleakly through the large and crispy hole in the seat of the chalk-striped trousers he was holding up before his face.

'Look at 'em!' Compo wailed. 'Hole as big as a toilet seat.'

'Maybe you can have it invisibly mended,' the sympathetic Clegg said without conviction.

'Tha could drive a bus through it,' Compo groaned. 'The long pillock! Him and his crappy machine. Look at me trousers!'

'Dry though, aren't they?' Seymour pointed out ill-advisedly and ducked as Compo launched himself over the back of Seymour's seat. Clegg hauled the whirling Long Johns back. I wouldn't do this for just anybody, he was thinking. Barry brought the car back on track from the path of a decorated lorry on its way to the Grand Float Parade. It was dressed as the shoe of the Old Woman Who Lived in a Shoe. The driver glared hard at them from the buckle as he passed and hooted angrily.

'Get out of it!' Compo gestured and shouted. He yelled from his window. 'If tha's a boot get theesen back on the pavement.'

Barry's pulse was going like a hamster on a treadmill. 'I'm beginning to appreciate,' he was blinking, trying to eyelash wipe the perspiration from his glasses, 'why Our Glenda's never very keen to see you lot commandeer her father.'

'So she sent thee instead,' Compo pointed out. 'That should make thee think a bit, young Barry.'

My God he's right Barry realised and went deathly quiet.

'Barry's quiet,' Clegg said.

'He's allus quiet,' Compo said.

'Makes a nice change,' Seymour announced sulkily. 'From some people who spend their lives nit-picking and moaning.'

'Moaning?' Compo began displaying again the wide open spaces where quantities of trouser used to be. 'Tha puts a patio door where me breeches arse should be. I should think I am moaning.'

'Oh stop going on so. I'll get you back to the gala in respectable condition. Why do you think I'm taking you to Rank Arnold's?'

'Rank Arnold scraps old bangers,' Compo spluttered. 'He's not going to have spare parts for what I'm missing.'

Seymour tapped his temple, complacently. 'I have it all worked out. Just leave it with me.'

'What's tha think he's going to do?' Compo persisted. 'I'm not bending down to be chuffin' welded.'

'We know he's not going to the gala,' Seymour explained. 'Owing to his mortal fear of the Incredible Female Hulk he's living-in-sin with.'

'Only partially living-in-sin,' Clegg felt the urge to be fair. 'Mostly he seems to be living in the back of an old Humber.

165

The wages of sin,' he winced for Rank Arnold, 'is living in the back of an old Humber.' It's true he realised. That's how diluted the old certainties have become.

'What I want to know,' Barry sounded thoroughly depressed, 'is why – if she can't trust you lot with her dad – did Glenda send me, her husband, instead?'

'Just lucky I guess,' Compo patted Barry's shoulder.

'As I was saying,' an indignant Seymour frowned, 'before I was interrupted. We are heading for Rank Arnold's because – One – we know he's not going to the gala. Two – ' he glared at Compo. 'He's about your size, therefore Three – you can borrow his best suit.'

It was an idea so startling that they had to mull it over for a hundred yards in silence. Rank Arnold, as a local figure of such grotty renown, had never entered their wildest imaginings as a potential source of even emergency tailoring.

'One has to improvise,' Seymour added, a trifle miffed at the flat reception for his brainwave.

'Wow!' Clegg whistled under his breath. 'Rank Arnold's best suit. That really is improvising.'

'Has he got a best suit?' Compo enquired. 'I've only ever seen him in overalls.'

'Filthy overalls,' Clegg corrected.

'Filthy overalls,' Compo agreed.

'Then his best suit must be practically unworn,' Seymour insisted with implacable logic. 'It must be like new.'

'But he's such a scruff,' Compo pointed out not unfairly.

'True,' Seymour admitted. 'So you see – as well as both being of the same height – that's something else you have in common.'

'I don't see why not,' Rank Arnold did some rapid calculations while scratching under his greasy trilby with a horny fingernail. 'Let's see. I could let you have the overnight loan of it at the same rate I charge for hiring out me special tools.'

'Money grabber,' Compo frowned. 'Is tha going to charge me so much a mile?'

166

Rank Arnold chuckled happily at the notion. They followed him into the living van. Barry remained behind, pacing the corroding alleys, wondering where he might have gone wrong in his marriage. Is it because I'm boring he wondered? I bet it is. I bet it's because I'm boring.

The living van interior made the scrapyard seem neat.

'She dun't go big licks on doing housework then, your bird,' Compo commented.

'No,' Rank Arnold admitted sorrowfully. 'She's purely for pleasure.'

They blinked a bit at that.

'Used to be like a little palace in here when your missis had it,' Compo persisted.

'I know,' Rank Arnold sighed. 'I lay awake many a night in the back of that Humber. Toying with exciting visions of the way the wife used to be flying around with the Jif and the Windowlene.' He clutched the startled Seymour, looking for a fresh, unbiased opinion. 'Do you think it's weird,' he demanded, 'for a bloke my age to be fantasising about going back to his wife?'

'Get him off!' Seymour pleaded. 'His hands are rusty.'

They detached Rank Arnold gently from his piece of Seymour. 'Why did tha leave thee wife?' Compo asked.

'I was looking for magic,' Rank Arnold confessed. 'I was fifty years old. A power in the scrap trade but there was no magic.'

'And where did tha meet this bird tha's living with?'

'She was in the trade. She came out of nowhere one rainy Saturday, with this beautiful load of old washing machines.'

'Wow!' Clegg said. 'That's some magic.'

'I thought – here it is,' Rank Arnold sighed. 'Me own Golden Girl. It wasn't just lust. I thought here it is at last. Somebody I can spend the long nights talking non-ferrous metals with. A partnership welded in heaven. Me Tarzan and there she was. Jane. The Scrap Merchant's Mate.'

'If we could just see the suit.' Seymour was looking at his watch.

Rank Arnold waved the interruption aside. In that confined and littered space he had what amounted to a

167

captive audience and he was determined to make the best of it. 'What's your hurry? Make yourselves at home,' he said. 'Sit down.'

'Where?' they asked.

'Feel about,' he said. 'Move a few things. There's some chairs somewhere.'

Outside, in the scrapyard, Barry was looking at his watch. He frowned at the living van. What are they doing in there, he wondered. Come on. Come on. But the door remained obstinately closed. It's time I was back, he announced to the empty scrapyard. Glenda's going to be whittling where I am. Or is she, he wondered? Does she care? It's her who sent me where her father fears to tread. He glared at Arnold's van. Among that lot. How long are they going to be? I've got to get back to the gala, he decided. Tackle Glenda. Find out exactly where I stand. Ask her how come I'm expendable all of a sudden. How come when there's a threat from this dozy mob she saves her father and abandons me? It's not that I've anything against her father. He's been a great source of comfort while I was having trouble with me starter motor. But I've got to know where I stand.

He was perspiring in the heat of midday. He wiped his glasses on a snowy handkerchief, his amiable, unlined, still puppy-plump face squinting in the scrapyard sunlight. He could smell long stagnant oil and decomposing metal.

I bet it's because I'm boring. He put his glasses back on. The world's matt finish returned to gloss. Married less than a year ago, I've bored her already. On the other hand if we've lasted nearly a year I can't be all that boring.

Yes I can, he decided. If she was just being nice about it. Hoping it might go away. It won't though. He sighed and poked with his toe at an old steering wheel on the ground. I can't help it, he told a sparrow bathing in the dust a few dead cars away. Inside I'm not boring I'm just quiet but I know how it looks from the outside. I see people's eyes glaze. But is

168

it grounds for divorce? If she goes will I still be able to take me problems to her father? Especially that starter motor. I'll be more forceful with her. Decisive. That's what they like. I will. I'll tell her, Look here, Glenda, I forbid you to leave me till I get a new starter motor.

He giggled nervously and looked at his watch again. I will. I'll be more decisive. I'll show her. I'll roust this mob out of that caravan for a start.

He strode decisively towards the van. He applied his ear to the flimsy door. He heard the clink of glasses. 'Oh no,' he groaned. He made a few small circuits on the oil-stained ground. Be decisive he challenged himself. He hammered on the door with a suddenly resolute fist.

'We're closed!' Rank Arnold bawled.

'Sorry,' the retreating Barry apologised.

'The suit,' Seymour interrupted Rank Arnold's flow of re-miniscence. 'Could we see the suit?'

They were seated now amid the debris drinking Rank Arnold's Home Brew from jam jars on account of his bird having political principles incompatible with fancy glasses. Rank Arnold frowned at this latest impoliteness from Seymour. 'What's the gallop? Is he always in such a gallop, your mate?'

'Always,' Clegg said.

'Gets on thee wick,' Compo sympathised.

'If we're ever going to get back to the gala,' Seymour pointed to his multi-function watch.

'That's a right machine is that,' Rank Arnold admired the watch, seizing Seymour's wrist the better to do so. 'It's got more buttons than me trouser fly.'

'I was expecting a zip,' the suddenly doubt-ridden Compo confessed.

'Who the hell's going to put a zip on a watch?' Rank Arnold asked.

'I mean on thee trouser fly,' Compo explained. 'Going back

169

to buttons, man, that's not very Space Age. How old is this suit?'

'It's in very good nick,' Rank Arnold said with injured pride. 'Never mind how old it is.'

'As long as it covers him up,' Seymour said. 'Hides those appalling Long Johns.'

'What's wrong with his Long Johns?' Rank Arnold enquired in genuine puzzlement as he studied the garments on Compo's flanks.

'The colour,' Seymour prompted.

Rank Arnold shrugged. 'Mine are that colour. I thought everybody's went that colour.'

Seymour gave it up.

Compo cackled happily.

Rank Arnold went to fetch the suit.

Barry heard the van door opening and appeared from behind the car. Seymour and Clegg stepped from the van followed by Rank Arnold. They turned back to face the door, waiting for the last of their little party. The doorway remained tantalisingly empty.

'Come along,' Seymour ordered.

'It's a bit tight,' Compo's voice answered. 'I'm coming. I'm coming.'

He appeared in the doorway. Barry gaped. Compo was trussed in the stifling embrace of a plum-coloured, two-piece suit plus an equally restrictive fancy waistcoat in Regency stripes. The whole outfit was cut in the Teddy Boy high style of the 'fifties.

'If it's too tight,' Rank Arnold suggested, 'forget it. Take it off. Try somebody else.'

'It's not too tight,' Compo lied gamely in a squeaky over-corsetted voice, which he hurriedly lowered an octave or two. 'Snug but amazingly comfy really.' He manufactured an unconvincing air of relaxation. He fancied the outfit like mad and he wasn't going to be parted. He could see himself twirling Nora at the gala dance. Well – maybe not twirling but certainly moving gracefully together crabwise. Sideways is easier, he was discovering. It's the fore and aft that brings the pain.

170

He moved sideways in the doorway and stretched a foot cautiously, feeling for the step. They took pity on him and lifted him down.

'Are you sure it's all right?' a concerned Clegg enquired.

'It's great, Norm,' Compo lied. 'Now tha's got me down on the level I'm fine.' He did a few fancy demo steps to convince them.

They saw his eyes water. They took hold of him and walked him gently towards the car.

It wouldn't start. Barry was blushing furiously at the clapped-out noises coming from under the bonnet each time he turned the key.

'It's your starter motor,' Rank Arnold diagnosed. 'As luck will have it I can find you one very reasonable. Fitting's extra,' he added, producing a spanner from his pocket. 'But if you leave it with me I'll have you back mobile in a couple of hours.'

'We haven't time to wait here two hours,' Seymour protested.

'Rush rush rush,' Rank Arnold sighed.

'Can't you give us a lift back to the gala,' Seymour suggested. 'Then you can work on the car here and we'll pick it up later.'

'Lifts are extra,' Rank Arnold warned as he walked away to collect his vehicle.

'You're quiet,' Clegg said to Compo.

'Don't bother me,' Compo pleaded. 'While I'm learning to wear this suit.'

Barry was looking worried. 'I think maybe somebody ought to ask him how much it's going to cost, this new starter motor.'

'It's a secondhand, scrap starter motor,' Seymour encouraged. 'Can't be all that costly, can it?'

Barry still looked worried.

They heard Rank Arnold's diesel clatter into life in one of the sheds. They saw a cloud of smoke reverse from the shed. It cleared to reveal an ancient, battered breakdown pick-up. Rank Arnold drove it towards them and braked. They backed away hastily from its idling fumes. Rank Arnold leaned out

171

from his cab. 'You'll have to climb up and stand in the back. There's no seats in here.'

They were staring at the grease and grime of a scrapyard lifetime covering every inch of the old work-horse vehicle. Rank Arnold saw their hesitation. 'You'll be all right,' he promised. 'You can hold on to the crane. My missis has travelled miles back there. Holding on to the crane.' Rank Arnold sighed nostalgically. 'She used to like a drive on a Sunday afternoon did my Millie.'

'I'm not riding up there in this new suit,' Compo announced flatly. 'I'm not turning up in front of Nora Batty covered in diesel. When I make me entrance, mate, I'm going to make an impression.' They watched in alarm as he began stripping off the suit. He folded it neatly and handed it up to Rank Arnold in the cab. 'Hang on to that for me, Arnold. I'll put it back on when we get there.'

His limbs celebrating their return to freedom in the baggy Long Johns, Compo climbed nimbly into the back of the pick-up.

Seymour was gaping at this scandalous, very off-white vision as it leaned casually against the crane.

'Well come on then,' the vision said. 'Chop chop. Get thee finger out.'

'You can't travel through a built-up area in that condition!' Seymour was outraged.

'Tha can all stand round me. Who the hell's going to see me? They'll all have gone off to watch the big float parade.'

'Your meter's ticking,' Rank Arnold warned. 'We're standing here gulping diesel.'

They climbed up reluctantly.

The town was deserted. In the back of the pick-up they began to relax. 'I told thee,' the grinning figure in his ash grey summer lightweights chortled, 'they'd all be watching the float parade. Hey up!' He stretched luxuriously. 'It's a treat this bit a breeze.'

172

'Don't do that,' Seymour pleaded as he clung to the crane. 'Tell him, Clegg, never to do that.'

'Do what?' Clegg enquired as he concentrated fiercely on trying to balance in the swaying vehicle. 'Oh that.'

'My God,' Seymour closed his eyes. 'He's doing it again.' Lord, he prayed silently, try not to let anyone of pedigree or social substance catch me under these reduced circumstances.

'Before I absolutely, definitively authorise a new second-hand scrap starter motor,' Barry confided into Clegg's wind-blown ear, 'I feel I ought to consult with Glenda. We always do everything together. At least we used to,' he sighed, 'Before she got bored.'

'Is Glenda bored?' Clegg shouted against the wind.

'Not so loud,' Barry winced.

Rank Arnold swung the pick-up round a corner and they were into flags and bunting and people lining the streets. The rear vehicle of the Grand Float Parade was just ahead, proceeding at a stately crawl. Rank Arnold was obliged to match its speed. The spectators, where the parade had passed, had been under the impression that the show was over and were now doubly delighted by this new source of entertainment. They cheered extravagantly.

The horrified Seymour blanched at the sight of all these happy, smiling faces. He bobbed down suddenly lusting after invisibility. This had the effect of revealing Compo to the crowd in all his glory. He crossed hands hastily over where he suddenly felt most exposed. The cheers of the crowd increased.

Seymour, still crouching and hiding his face with one hand pounded on the cab roof with the other.

'What can I do?' Rank Arnold shrugged helplessly. 'There's no place to turn round.'

'Reverse,' Seymour commanded. 'Back her up.' But when he looked behind, the crowd had spilled into the roadway and were following.

'You must be joking,' Rank Arnold jerked a thumb like a freshly dug parsnip at the pedestrians now almost in tow.

'All right, go forward,' Seymour extemporised. 'Overtake

173

the floats till you can turn off at the next junction. Put your foot down!'

Rank Arnold hooted and swung past the rear float. It was dressed as a castle. Two medieval maidens gaped as Compo drew alongside. The archer on the battlements was a Mister Cyril Bewmont of 'Eldorado', 24 Sugden Street who dreamed hard all year of this moment of glory when his military accoutrements showed bolder than his bald head or his paunch. And now here were some drunken, half-naked gypsies, threatening to turn the whole thing into farce.

Waving his longbow peremptorily and fixing them with the glare which cowed his customers at the Gas Board Show-rooms, he shouted above the chug of Rank Arnold's diesel, 'Back! Get back, man!'

It's Him-from-the-Gas-Board, Compo recognised as they carried on overtaking. A right bossy breeches.

Within seconds, it seemed, they overtook two more floats, occasioning between Rank Arnold and the other drivers much chit-chat of a kind not remarkable for its carefree gala spirit. But after a lifetime's free-booting in the junk trade Rank Arnold could hold his end up when it came to a bit of waspish badinage.

Seymour was wincing at the strength of one peppery passage when Rank Arnold stopped in mid-flow.

They were approaching the fourth float. It was that of the Rainbow Circle. Beneath a raised and decorated platform on which the Conjugal Wrights, in full competition magnifi-cence, were swaying Latinly together, were grouped the Lonely Hearts in their much plainer finery. A cassette player was throbbing out the music to which the Conjugal Wrights were dancing.

'For Friendship and Marriage,' the logo read, 'Join the Rainbow Circle.' A few of the Circlers were dancing to the music, pale echoes of those exotic movers on the platform, but most were ageing females, seated on former Sunday school chairs, clutching their handbags and looking embar-rassed. It was one of these, a plain, sturdy creature with ineptly applied lipstick who had stunned Rank Arnold into silence.

174

'Millie!' he bellowed, recovering full volume of his powers of speech. She was staring back, looking as if she was longing for a place to hide as his cab drew alongside. He was trying to lean through his nearside window. His steering became wildly unreliable. In the back they were hanging on to the crane. Those on the float had less support and were gazing in alarm as this piratical intruder kept swerving into what looked like a boarding position. The Conjugal Wrights kept dancing gamely but there was an out-of-tempo look creeping into their eyes.

'Millie,' Rank Arnold bellowed. 'What have you got on your face? Good God, lass! I turn me back two minutes and you start wearing lipstick. I won't have it. Behind me back. Wearing lipstick. All over your face. It's not good enough. Just 'cos I've left you for a while. I won't have it. And that's final. Is that understood?'

'You what?' said Millie. 'I can't hear for the music.'

'Oh stuff me!' Rank Arnold swerved wildly and began again.

'No,' said Seymour. 'Not again. You're blocking the road, man. You can't just strike up a conversation. You're a hazard. Do have a little thought for other road users. Get us out of here!'

'You what?' said Rank Arnold. 'I can't hear for the music.'

Seymour groaned.

'Come home, Millie,' Rank Arnold pleaded. 'Back to your little van. We'll throw me other bird out. We can do it. Together.'

Millie cupped a hand to her ear.

A motor-cycle policeman was at the junction ahead. Rank Arnold nosed in behind the Rainbow Circle float. They joined the parade.

At the gala field the mayor was waiting to judge the floats. Bean-Peach was fussing with the mike, tapping and testing and raising electronic howls which had the crowd reaching to cover their ears.

175

'He faffs about like a Tory,' the mayor confided to his wife.

'Keep your voice down,' she snapped, looking down at her husband's short, tubby figure. 'At least he's tall and slim with attractive grey hair.'

The mayor ran a hand across his balding head and sighed. He readjusted the hang of his chain. 'Margery,' he said, 'I sometimes wonder if you're altogether reliable politically.'

The crowd clapped the entry of the leading float into the field. Nora was on tiptoe peering over heads. 'They're coming,' she said.

'Great,' Wally acknowledged in tones of raging indifference.

Nora looked down at him, buried among the ranks of spectators. 'Can you see?'

'I'll jump,' he said, 'when we get to an exciting bit.'

She ignored him. She watched the leading floats arrive and joined the applause as they passed the mayor's stand. She heard the chuckling begin from the crowd on the flank. She saw the civic party looking perplexed. She saw the Conjugal Wrights looking furious as they tried to recapture the dignity of their dance while being followed by a grotty breakdown vehicle whose even grottier driver, his head through the window, was exchanging insults and pillow-talk in the loudest of voices with one of their own Rainbow Circlers.

The crowd applauded. Everybody loves a lover, Nora was thinking sentimentally and then she saw who was in the back of the pick-up. And in what condition! She gasped.

He saw her among the sea of faces and he waved. Which on reflection, he realised, could be a mistake. His hand shot back to its primary duty but it was too late. The crowd was giving him a great gala day salutation. He saw Nora covering her eyes and the bobbing head of Wally as he jumped.

'Well, you wanted to make an impression,' Clegg said. He removed his cap as they cruised past the startled mayoress and put it where it would do most good.

'Are we safe yet?' Seymour asked, his face buried as he lay on the floor.

176

'Tha can come out now,' Compo nudged Clegg.

Seymour rose.

It was hot in the beer tent. Early Taters removed his overcoat and by that simple act became apparently invisible. People who had known him since a lad showed him no recognition in his best suit.

Edie was keeping a passionate eye on her entry in the sponge-cake class. She had Wesley (who was pining for greener pastures) on guard at the other side of the trestle table, with instructions to intercept, on his side, all foreign intruders within the airspace of the cake: flies, creepy crawlies, elbows, handbags, and the fingers of competitors who were not beyond having a prod.

Ruby was selling honey from her own bees. Neatly jarred and labelled, it was going steadily. Her stall was trimmed festively with the stuff from her garden. Cosgrave, from the concealment of the crowd round the arm-wrestlers, was watching her blonde head bobbing busily. He felt cold lumps and pangs of pure regret.

Lady Georgina passed with the mayor in tow and Bean-Peach fussing in her ear. She caught the direction of her son's gaze. The girl looked like a worker at least.

The bandsmen were taking a beer break.

Barry went in search of his father-in-law and found him still standing sentry on Edie's cake. Barry smiled dutifully at his mother-in-law. 'Don't knock the table,' she warned.

Barry backed away hastily. He moved to the safer side of the apathetic Wesley who was suffering sensory deprivation from the lack of anything to tinker with.

'Wesley,' Barry said. 'Do you think your Glenda thinks I'm boring?'

'I expect so,' the only half attending Wesley said.

Barry sighed. That takes care of that then. O.K. Next question. 'Wesley, would you buy a secondhand starter motor from Rank Arnold?'

177

Offered this (if only theoretical) mechanical lifeline, Wesley's metabolism perked up. 'You'll have to argue price,' he warned. 'And for God's sake don't let him fix it. He's a big hammer merchant with absolutely no finesse.'

Seeing the sparkle of life returning to Wesley's eyes Barry was thinking – Well there you go then. Wesley doesn't find me boring. Perhaps if I talked to Glenda more. But is she interested in starter motors?

For the third year running, Nora won the Whitest Handkerchief Competition.

Bean-Peach found Rosemary at the home-made wine stall. 'There you are! Good heavens, woman, do you know what time it is? Why aren't you dressed for the chariot?' Wearing a blissful smile Rosemary advanced unsteadily towards her husband, plucked at his clerical waistband and began pouring inside it a bottle of Mrs Heptonstall's parsnip wine. I do believe, he realised, she's not fit to drive.

Early Taters, depressed by his new status of total stranger, had drunk himself into such a low that he began to seek the company of his wife. He found her at the bingo stall. 'It's as if I don't exist,' he complained. 'It's unnerving.'

'Tell him to have some hush,' the woman next to Mrs Early Taters snarled. 'Who is he anyway?'

'Don't ask me,' Mrs Early Taters said maliciously. 'Never seen him before.'

Edie won an Honourable Mention in the Sponge Cake Class. Wesley fled to safer territory.

Compo in Rank Arnold's Teddy Boy suit was finding it a tight squeeze on the dodgems. Seymour and Clegg had to lift him out. 'By hell!' he breathed through clenched teeth. 'Tha could feel every bump.'

178

There were fireworks in the evening and a floor laid for dancing.

The band had had several beer breaks, their tempo perhaps not quite to the exacting standards of the Conjugal Wrights.

Nobody else seemed to mind.

Rank Arnold, still in his overalls, was dancing with the former Mrs Rank Arnold.

Rank Arnold's best suit kept overtaking him with Nora Batty in his arms.

Nora was thinking – I was dreading this dance. He always asks me for a dance. What can you do? Though I must say, so far, he's behaving. Holding himself upright and stiffly. Quite like a gentleman.

Life, Compo was thinking, can be a bitch. Here I am finally wi' big handfuls of Nora Batty, my true love, and I'm snookered on account of tight tailoring. I daren't make a wrong move. I'd never make me getaway in this outfit.

I suppose sometimes he means well, Nora was remembering the peacock.

Oh what the hell! Compo decided. Escape's not everything.

From somewhere in the trees the peacock answered, as if challenged, the outraged squawk of Nora Batty.

Epilogue

Before morning the weather broke. Empty gala tents were percolated by a steady downpour. It drummed on the leads of the Hall and slapped wetly inside into containers sited for the purpose.

The peacock shook wet feathers in its tree. The gala debris lay saturated in the gala field. Paper and plastic; bottles and cans; the shards of coconut shells; crushed pellets of tinfoil; bits of Picknicker's Friends. An occasional photo-flash of lightning fixed for split seconds the wet and glossy scene.

It was fine again by dawn. The sky stayed overcast but the earth smelled strongly and sweet. The town rose perhaps a trifle laggardly to its morning after; creaked a shade woundedly back into gear. The hiss of Andrews or of Alka Seltzer competed with breakfast television.

It was mid-morning before they met up and walked a first mile in almost total silence. Compo in his own tatty clothing had been given back the free use of his limbs. He wished his head was feeling as nimble.

Seymour was bleeding from an unsteady shave. He dabbed at his throat with a paper handkerchief.

Clegg was dying for another cup of tea.

'Can you see any blood on my collar?' Seymour asked.

'Not this morning,' Clegg said hastily. 'Not without me glasses.'

Seymour thrust his neck Compowards.

'Tha'll have to bend down,' Compo said. 'I'm not into fancy head movements this mornin'.'

'Oh forget it!' a disgruntled Seymour conceded.

Barry made tea and took it up the heavily mortgaged stairs to Glenda. She woke to find him staring down at her. She reached up to feel his temperature. 'Whatever's the matter?'

'I'm boring, aren't I?'

She relaxed, vastly relieved. 'Is that all? Yes,' she conceded. 'We're both of us boring. Thank God. Them exciting marriages last about five minutes.'

Edie was alone in her kitchen in pursuit already of the ultimate sponge cake. Wesley could smell it in the shed. He sighed and began practising the sentiments of appreciation he knew would shortly be required of him. Teatimes were going to be tricky for a week or two.

Lady Georgina was rifling her library for every volume on bees. Damned if she was going to be outfaced altogether if he was to start bringing the girl to the house.

'Yesterday, Rosemary,' Bean-Peach accused at the breakfast table, 'in front of parishioners, you behaved inexcusably with a bottle of parsnip wine. I want to know why.'

'It was all I had,' Rosemary giggled despite a pounding head. 'They'd run out of elderberry.'

Bean-Peach had a foreboding that his life henceforward would never quite be the same.

The climb had burned off the gala excess. Appetite was returning.

181

'I could murder pie and peas,' Compo announced.

'You usually do,' Seymour said.

They began walking back to town. It was warm under the overcast. If I start sweating, Clegg wondered, does an alarm start clanging somewhere in the command module of the Armpit Millionaire?

Seymour was gazing down the valley. They're not ready round here for the Picnicker's Friend. To be quite blunt about it, they're still too good with their fingers. Upmarket – that's where I ought to be. Glyndebourne, Ascot – Henley

Compo was chuckling at a gala memory. Of Early Taters so low and defenceless that he allowed himself to be drafted at the last minute into driving a chariot for the vicar's Roman army. And so befuddled from his trips to the beer tent that, once he got the reins in his hand, he kept on automatically calling his wares: 'Organic veg. Get your lovely veg.' The star turn of the pageant. It brought the house down. He wasn't a stranger after that.

They quickened their paces homewards heading for pie and peas.